'THE CALL' GIRLS

'The Call' Girls

Tina Lesher

Information about contacting the author or purchasing copies of the novel is available at
theleshers.com

ISBN: 0692889493
ISBN 13: 9780692889497

INTRODUCTION

———————

WHEN MY CHILDREN WERE PRESCHOOLERS, I started writing this book on a typewriter and then stuck the initial few chapters away for decades in a large brown envelope. After resurrecting the work from a pile of things I kept over the years, I decided to update the material and finish what I started.

This time, I used a computer!

The result is *'The Call' Girls*, a novel about two young women who juggle motherhood with ownership of a small-town Connecticut weekly named The Dunfield Call.

My objective centered on telling a story within a context of humor. So I incorporated the oft-hilarious work of raising young children with the seriousness of engaging in credible journalism.

Though I never owned a paper, I did dabble for a number of years in the professional world of journalism and later moved to academia as a journalism professor.

As for motherhood: well, my three offspring will have to judge me in that category!

Please enjoy *'The Call' Girls*.

CHAPTER 1

———

ALMOST WITHOUT EFFORT, HANK WATSON hoisted his grimacing spouse, Janet, from their aging Jeep Grand Cherokee and carried her through the emergency room door at St. Mark's Hospital in Dunfield, a town outside of Hartford.

"Another novice skier," boomed the obese nurse, much like an announcer at ringside. "Wow, and a pregnant one at that."

At least my figure is temporary, thought Janet as she eyed the oversized Florence Nightingale and said "I think my ankle is broken. Maybe sprained."

"How'd you swing that, honey? On the slopes?" asked the nurse.

"No, a turkey fell on it."

A muffled ripple of laughter raced through the nurses' station. Even Janet recognized the humor in the situation. She had opened the freezer at the top of the refrigerator to remove some frozen pizzas for dinner. In shuffling things about the crowded compartment, she inadvertently uprooted a 12-pound frozen turkey that quickly jetted onto her slippered foot.

The pain was beginning to outweigh the humor as Hank dutifully answered the receptionist's questions about his wife.

"Age?"

"She's 34," answered Hank.

"Occupation?"

"Free-lance writer. Emphasis on FREE."

The nursing staff, buzzing over the unusual circumstances surrounding Janet's injury, ignored any real attempt to treat her for well over an hour.

"For Christ's sake," bellowed Hank, "will someone help her?"

"We're getting there," warbled the blubbery nurse, turning to a befuddled-looking aide and ordering her to "get Mrs. Watson some ice for her ankle."

"Where's the ice?" asked the aide as she looked toward the nurse.

Before the latter could answer, Janet cried out: "You don't know where the ice is?"

"I just started here 10 minutes ago," the aide responded.

The scene was beginning to resemble an Abbott and Costello routine. A nurses' aide, just starting her first shift on the job, was taking orders from a bulging, sergeant-like supervising nurse, while an embarrassed patient, just into her third month of pregnancy, painfully exhibited an ankle injury incurred when a two-month-old frozen turkey fell out of the freezer.

My whole life resembles a comedy scene, thought Janet as she posed while two male X-ray technicians photographed her swollen foot.

She had traded a budding career as a sportswriter, one of few women to pursue that end of the newspaper business, for a role as wife of a Harvard Business School graduate who made his living as a banker.

That term made her cringe. Hank wavered in middle management in a loan officer's post at Hartford Bank and, unlike wives of some of his coworkers, she couldn't bring herself to refer to him as a "banker." After all, she'd argue, why aren't tellers called bankers?

For Janet, motherhood proved more productive than anticipated.

"This your first child?" asked one radiology technician as his colleague gently turned Janet sideways to X-ray the other side of her left foot.

"No. This is number three."

"How old are the others?"

"1 and 2."

"She's either crazy or Catholic," he opined to his cohort.

"Neither," said Janet. "And, unlike you two, I enjoy what I'm doing in life."

"What makes you think we don't?" asked one.

"Oh, I can see **right through** you two X-ray guys," she answered to the shocked laughter of the radiology technicians.

If one thing had carried Janet Denis Watson through life, it was her remarkably quick wit.

When Hank knelt on one knee to pop the marriage question, she grabbed a Post-It and wrote: "You KNEED me?"

Once, when then-Red Sox coach Don Zimmer alluded in an interview to his attempt to shed extra poundage, Janet said audibly: "I think your diet is PASTA DUE" as her fellow sportswriters roared.

Now a middle-age paunchy physician, with X-rays in hand, approached Janet back in the emergency room and reported: "No break. Bad sprain. Keep ice on it tonight. Use crutches for a few days or so. Take aspirin."

That was it. The doctor simply read the X-rays. He never even inquired as to how Janet felt. Though in obvious pain, Janet giggled as she peered at an overhead sign: "Physician's Fee: $300.

She turned to Hank: "we have to pay this MD a few hundred bucks to read an X-ray and utter a few words. Plus we have emergency room costs, radiology charges, and babysitting fees. All because your mother decided not to come to dinner two months ago and I put the dumb turkey in the freezer."

The rookie nurses' aide arrived with crutches in hand. She wished the mother-to be "good luck."

"You're the one who needs it in this place," smiled Janet. "By the way, how long do I get to keep these crutches?"

The overstuffed nurse supervisor, hearing Janet's question, yelled: "You don't borrow… you have to buy them."

"Really," laughed Janet. "Do they come in maternity sizes?"

CHAPTER 2

———

Hobbling to the ringing phone proved no easy task for Janet, especially with two dynamos tugging at her sweatshirt.

"Good afternoon," she answered cheerfully, forgetting she had cleaned up the cereal from the kids' regular breakfast fiasco and that it was just after 9 a.m.

"Dr. Singer's office," stated the voice, recognizably that of the physician's receptionist. "Did you forget your appointment?"

In the wake of dealing with her oversized ankle, Janet failed to remember that the obstetrician wanted her to have a sonogram to determine why her impregnated middle was protruding so quickly.

"Oh cripes, I forgot. But my cleaning lady is coming any minute and she can watch my children so can I come then?"

"Sure."

A little while later, Janet slowly entered the doctor's office and put her crutches aside as she lay down to have the sonogram.

"Mrs. Watson, you have children who are ages 1 and 2-and-a-half, right?" the doctor inquired as he studied the screen.

"Is this a survey or shocking news?" laughed Janet.

"Well, it looks like twins."

Janet's ears popped; her mouth plummeted to pelican position.

She wanted to grab the list of physicians in the large practice and look up "cardiologist." She figured she might as well call before she had a heart attack.

Dr. Singer continued: "Everything looks fine. They'll be good-sized babies, no doubt."

No one had to tell Janet that she would deliver big offspring. She'd already given birth to two 10-pound babies.

At different times.

All she kept muttering was: "Four kids under three years of age. Oh, my God."

She once had been threatened verbally by an angry Boston Bruins wing about whom she editorialized in her weekly column: "His poor play of late reflects his apparent unwillingness to scramble. He should get his teeth into the act."

She had forgotten he lacked his two front teeth.

The feeling that rocked her the following day, when the hockey star issued a threat to HER teeth, appeared minor to the shock resulting from Dr. Singer's news.

Now at home and holding the crutches, she shakily guided herself onto the sprawling recliner that Hank had purchased as a birthday present---for himself---and propped her foot on the attached ottoman. Staring at her from the television was a re-run of the canceled soap opera, "All My Children."

"All MY children," she barked at the TV set.

Marta, a playful and cheery child whose third birthday was a few months away, tackled a toy project on the den floor, while 13-month-old Molly fought a playpen nap in the adjacent living room.

"How will I tell your father?" Janet repeatedly muttered to her uninterested daughters. She mulled novel ways to break the news to Hank, who was flabbergasted at the thought of ONE more baby in the household.

Janet considered handing him a stiff martini the moment he came home.

One drink and he'd see double.

Her thoughts terminated with the sound of the doorbell and the arrival of her longtime friend, Kitty McIntyre. "Thought I could take Marta for the afternoon so you could rest your battered ankle," announced Kitty with a supportive look on her face. "First, however, I will stay for a late lunch. I bought some tuna grinders at the deli."

"A double egg sandwich would be more appropriate," snickered Janet as she suddenly burst into song: "Four in the bed and the little one said Roll over, roll over...so they all rolled over and one fell out...three in the bed...

"Maybe you ought to go to bed," commented a puzzled Kitty.

"Go ahead, Kits, tell me I remind you of the late Kate Smith. The figure and the voice are perfecto."

She was alluding to the heavyset singer who several decades before became famous for singing "God Bless America" at The Flyers' games at The Spectrum in Philly.

"I hate hockey," said Kitty.

"You'd love it if Tim were the team dentist," remarked Janet as Kitty cracked up.

Kitty, too, was a newswoman-turned-homemaker-of-sorts, a copy editor who sported a reputation of being top-notch in her fielding. Her clever headlines had landed her a number of prizes in state competition. Kitty scrapped her fulltime post on the Hartford Tribune four years previously when she and her dentist-spouse became parents of Timmy. To retain her skills, however, she filled in two nights a week on the Trib copydesk.

"Oh," said Kitty, "when I dropped Timmy at nursery school this afternoon, I ran into Jenny Hensell---remember her from St. Agnes? She asked me how you were doing these days. I said, 'Janet has two toddlers and another baby on the way. I don't think Jenny could believe it.'"

"Two," said Janet.

"Two what?"

"Two on the way."

A bewildered Kitty did not grasp the remark; she stared blankly as she munched on the tuna sandwich.

Returning to her impromptu songfest, Janet started mumbling "Tea for Two and two for tea..."

She stopped abruptly.

"Twins, Kitty. Dr. Singer did the sonogram this morning and said I'm carrying twins."

"Jiminy Jesus," bellowed Kitty. "I thought you looked big."

"I could write a story about myself---ex-sportswriter who's the best in her sport. The Olympic contender in conception."

"And I'll write the headline," interrupted Kitty as she scribbled on a leftover Yuletide napkin. "How about: Sportswriter Lands Olympic BIRTH."

"Do they give a higher degree-of-difficulty for twins?" asked Janet. "Can you imagine Kitty, I covered five Super Bowls, took batting practice with the Yankees and got hit with a shanked Tiger Woods drive, and here I rest with a lousy ankle and bambinos three and four protruding from my frame. And to think my mother gave me the middle name of Mary after the Blessed Mother. The only thing we have in common is the stable. She was there and I am not!"

The newswomen/moms laughed uproariously.

At least I can chuckle about it, mused Janet to herself. A few months back, she and Hank had decided to put any thoughts of more children on the back burner. At Dr. Singer's suggestion, Janet agreed to use an IUD for birth control. Upon learning of her pregnancy, she promptly labeled the device as It's Usually Defective.

As she shared a noontime respite with her friend, Janet mentally recalled the time at Fenway Park when she opted out of her usual spot in the Red Sox press box and covered a weekend series against the Yankees from the bleachers beyond the famous Green Wall. The experience netted her a chance to mingle with the die-hard Bosox fans and to pen a humorous, but sentimental first-page piece about "Life in the (Fenway) Suburbs." The article took top prize in a national sports reporting contest; the framed piece was among the prize-winning stories adorning the extra bedroom that Janet used as an office.

"Kate, Kate Smith, what's for dessert?" asked Kitty of the deep-in-thought Janet.

"How about one little, two little, three little Indian pudding? Oops... Four little..."

They continued to laugh as Kitty suddenly interjected:" What's Hank's reaction to the news about the twins?"

"Hank---oh, my god. I have to tell him."

CHAPTER 3

———

HANK WATSON, A UPENN GRADUATE, put in a stint with the Teach America program before working at a Framingham bank for a few years. Then he headed to Harvard Business School for his MBA. While there, he met Janet Denis at a party near the Cambridge campus.

After receiving a journalism degree from the highly touted University of Missouri School of Journalism, Janet penned sports stories for four years at The Philadelphia Inquirer before leaving to pursue a graduate degree in communications at Boston University. To pay her bills, she put in 12 hours a week shoveling press releases for a local hospital.

"I'm the queen of CAT scan stories" she would tell her BU classmates.

From Hank's perspective, courting never encompassed more than three dates with a girl because the ones he met always bored him with their talk of careers or marriage. He hesitated to take a date to a sporting event after one experience when he brought a young woman to a basketball game. At one point, he turned to her and lamented: "too many turnovers tonight."

She responded gleefully: "Oh, do they sell them at the concession stand?"

Hank's attraction to the petite Janet Denis appeared grounded not in her physical attributes (although her black, pixie hair and constant smile acted as lures), but in her wit, her conversation, and her knowledge of sports. At the party where they met, Hank listened in fascination as Janet and another guest discussed rising salaries in the National Basketball Association.

Janet made it clear from the start that she abhorred marriage, children, and suburbia, but Hank discovered her weakness---flowers---and when single, long-stem roses appeared at her door every day for a fortnight, she was ready to accept an offer of marriage.

They exchanged vows three months later in Old North Church, Boston, and honeymooned in Nantucket before setting up housekeeping in two states. Hank continued his final semester at Harvard and lived in a graduate dorm there while Janet, who had completed graduate school, took a sportswriting job at The Hartford Tribune and resided in their rented Newington, Ct. townhouse; Hank weekended there until he completed his degree.

That was six years ago, Hank reflected as he removed his sneakers after a workout at the local Y. Kitty's spouse, Tim McIntyre, had joined Hank in the locker room and the pair was making small talk about their personal lives.

"Kitty told me the news about the twins on the way. How did Janet break that news to you?"

"She knew I would go into shock so she wrote me a note when I was downing a beer the other night."

"What'd it say?" asked Tim.

"It said: Two Be or Not Two Be. That is the question. TO was spelled TWO. I said: What the hell is this? That is not how you spell To Be or Not To Be. She said Yes it is and pointed to her expanding belly. I got the message. And I dropped the beer on the floor."

Tim smirked: "You don't look overjoyed, Hank."

"Well, my checkbook and my sanity cannot tolerate four little ones too easily."

Hank remained pensive for a week or so after hearing the news. He worried about finances, career competition, mental strain---and the lawn!

The Watsons' new split-level in Dunfield, a Hartford suburb, featured an acre-long mudfield when they arrived shortly after Molly's birth. Hank seeded, watered, fertilized and limed the back area, which Janet christened Boss Weed. Her spouse once threatened to gravel the entire yard.

"A dime for your thoughts," Janet smiled one night after Hank had invested hours in pulling weeds on the struggling lawn.

"A dime?"

"Inflation, honey."

"That is what bothers me. Inflation, not the damn yard. Money is the root of all marital strife. Too much of it translates into a ticket for overlooking the important things. Too little and it destroys anything you can make of a situation. Just enough and you worry because you can't figure out why the hell you're just making it."

Their regular bantering ensued.

"Hank, I didn't ask for this. I was content in my own career. I never longed for housekeeping, dirty diapers, budgets---or a bunch of little kids."

"Christ, here we go again. I dragged you down---all my fault. OK, I'll get a teaching job at night. What don't you string for that local yokel weekly? That way we'll get a few extra bucks."

"OK, but you'll have to watch the kids if I cover municipal meetings and when..."

She stopped in mid-sentence. The sound of organ music filtered through the neighborhood.

"Where is that coming from?" barked Hank.

"Phil Rankin---the guy in the new house on the corner," said Janet. "He has a big organ."

"How the hell do you know?" said her spouse.

They laughed their way out of the conversation.

CHAPTER 4

———

AFTER FOUR STRAIGHT HOURS OF reading and editing a six-part series on local architecture, including one piece devoted to unusual bathrooms in the Hartford area ("better set the headline flush right," yelled the copydesk chief), Kitty McIntyre stopped for a coffee break. It was 9 p.m. and she was scheduled to work until midnight when the second edition would be "put to bed," as they say in newspaper lingo.

She sauntered to a nearby phone and dialed Janet Watson.

"It's just me, Jan," she explained to the mother-to-be. "Feeling okay?"

"I feel like a pachyderm," said Janet. "I have so many varicose veins in my leg that I look like a road Atlas. My ankles are swelling, I think, but I can't see them."

"Whoa---what else is new, Momma?"

"I spent the day making Christmas cookies."

"In May?"

"I thought it would be a kick. I'll be too busy with four kids to bake them in December."

"So you'll freeze them?"

"I ate them. I had this craving to devour the little Christmas trees. I think I'm out of my tree, Kits. Of course, I decided to bake after two hours of playing Candyland with Marta. I should start a blog, Kitty. It'll be the same thing every day--up, eat, wash, dust, TV talk shows, nap, Candyland, dinner, etc. I can write 'ditto' every day."

"You sound a bit down, Janet. And I have good news for you."

"Hit me."

"The new living page editor, Martha Fox, is looking for a columnist to write things of interest to mothers and I guess women in general. Williams suggested you."

"Williams suggested me? He must be off the wagon again," said the ex-Tribune sportswriter.

Jack Williams was the aging, beer-belting sports editor for whom Janet had worked at the paper. His bout with the booze had cost him his wife and his health; he always seemed to have some type of ailment.

Williams griped constantly about the female segment of society. When he learned that the Trib managing editor had hired Janet to join the all-male sports staff, he headed for a three-day binge.

Kitty continued: "I understand Williams said to Martha Fox yesterday: 'If it's a mother you want, I know the perfect one. Not the perfect mother. The perfect writer.'"

"It sounds like Jack," laughed Janet, who during her Tribune years had won the respect of Williams along with her score of writing awards.

"Anyway, Janet, call Martha tomorrow. I gotta run. The lead story is waiting."

And thus was conceived the humor-packed, often topical weekly column, "Oh, Mother!"

Janet chose the title herself after considering a host of other possibilities including "The Mom Beat." As Kitty said: "Putting the word Beat with Mom in this day and age is a no-no; they might take it out of the newspaper context and haul you off for verbal assault!"

The column, which Janet wrote from home, proved successful, by most standards.

When she wittingly opined that housewives should be unionized ("If anyone knows the labor movement, it's moms"), the Tribune was besieged with emails and letters from supportive mothers.

When she sarcastically condemned a panty hose firm for sponsoring a two-mile run ("that's appropriate considering the size of the ones in their products"), she won the plaudits of scores of pantyhose wearers, although The Tribune had a difficult time retaining the manufacturer's ads.

Spurred by a wire story alluding to teenage promiscuity, she dashed off a column titled: "Don't Go to Bed Until You're Wed." Letters to the editor and e-mails flooded The Tribune as parents praised her, feminist groups blasted her, and one grandmotherly type wrote: "Mrs. Watson truly realizes that the beauty of procreation rests in the love shared by a husband and wife."

"I surely know about procreation," Janet remarked as she read the missive aloud to a group of Trib reporters one Indian summer night when she was a few weeks away from her due date. Although her stories were sent by computer from her home, she tried to stop at the paper at least once a week to pick up snail mail and discuss potential ideas for upcoming columns.

Her arrival this particular evening was marked by a present from the editor: a basket filled with letters from "Oh, Mother" readers.

Friends on the staff laughed heartily as she read some of the letters in the Tribune cafeteria.

"Would you bowl with us and write a funny story?' asked the Spare Tireds in a letter to which Janet commented: "Sure, I look like a bowling ball these days."

One woman wrote: "I loved your column that suggested establishing Housekeepers Anonymous. I want to join so when I feel like cleaning I can call another member and she will talk me out of it."

"You remind me of jai-lai," a man wrote without explaining why.

Her newspaper cronies chuckled repeatedly. Then, as she reached for more letters and copies of e-mails sent to the paper, Janet stopped suddenly and cried out: "Oh, my God."

She grimaced in pain.

"What's wrong?' asked Al Evans, the Trib medical writer who had known Janet since they toiled together on the Philadelphia Inquirer.

"My water just broke. Do something, Al."

"Jesus, not me," said the pale-faced Evans. "I'll call one of the business reporters…they're working on a labor story."

"This isn't funny," a serious Janet announced. "Get me to St. Mark's Hospital."

With four reporters accompanying her, the pain-faced Janet Watson entered St. Mark's emergency room. She immediately recalled her last time there---several months earlier when she had been smashed by the frozen turkey. Her ankle still ached a bit, she realized, but then so did every other part of her blimp-shaped physique.

"Baby?" asked the receptionist.

"No, hemorrhoids," answered Jack Williams, the sarcastic sports editor who insisted on being among the group escorting the "Oh, Mother" columnist to the hospital.

"Why aren't they treating that man over there?' asked medical writer Evans as he pointed to the gentleman obviously suffering from breathing problems.

The staff ignored Al's inquiry as the receptionist continued questioning Janet. "Name and doctor?"

"Janet Watson and Singer."

"Sounds like a great name for a group," commented Liz Ames, the entertainment writer who said "I want to see this show" as her colleagues whisked Janet from the Trib newsroom.

Everything happened so quickly that, even months later, Janet could not recount much about the evening. Tales from her accompanying reportorial entourage---they coauthored the next "Oh, Mother" with details---indicated that Janet had fainted into police reporter Fred Smith's arms, been rushed to the delivery room and given birth to twin boys even before Hank made it to the hospital.

The loudly cheering reporters were escorted from the waiting room, but not until Al Evans threatened to write an article on emergency room care, "or lack of it," as he hollered to the chief physician.

Kitty arrived at the hospital the following afternoon with four carnations.

"Two pink. Two blue. Now a mom of four are you!" read the card.

"The babies are gorgeous," she told Janet, who was overjoyed that the new offspring, each weighing close to five pounds at birth, were smiling and happy. "Boys are a joy," laughed Kitty, "But they cost more right from the start."

"They do?

"Wait until you get the bill for two circumcisions."

"Cripes," argued Janet. "I don't want to make a flap over it."

Kitty roared: "That is hilarious! I swear you should be a stand-up comic."

CHAPTER 5

———

THE SALVATION FOR MOMS IS Mothers Morning Out, wrote Janet one week in her "Oh, Mother!" column. She was alluding to a program, sponsored by the Dunfield Congregational Church, which offered care one morning each week to infants and preschoolers. The objective simply was to provide a break for a few hours for young mothers.

When the Watson quartet---Marta, Molly, Bret and Billy---would arrive each Wednesday, the program director would smile.

"Who else would smile at the arrival of four screaming siblings?" asked Janet in her column.

On one free Wednesday morning, Janet made haste to the Main Street offices of the town's weekly newspaper, The Dunfield Call. The name was a joke among those educated in journalism.

"It isn't what I'd CALL a newspaper," Janet would say on almost any occasion when the weekly's articles were being discussed. Nonetheless, Dunfielders and others in the area digested the publication with the hopes of finding their names or those of their soccer-playing offspring. Whatever stories arrived at the paper were put into print, many times sporting the same spelling or grammatical errors from the original copy.

Janet's visit to The Call this day resulted from an almost begging-like request from Rev. John Smythe to handle newspaper publicity for his St. Matthew's Episcopal Church. Janet, who had been a member of the congregation since her childhood, felt compelled to accept.

"They kept preying on me to do it," she told Kitty. "Now they better pray that I do it."

The church was set to launch a fundraising campaign in hopes of securing enough monies for a teen center; Janet was hand-delivering a press release about the start of the drive. She knew she could have emailed the release but felt it would be more beneficial to speak to an editor about the money-raising campaign.

"It reads well," said Clara Woodruff, the matronly-looking editor, as she perused Janet's release.

Clara knew about Janet's journalistic background and automatically placed the latter's articles on The Call's front page. This proved a boon for Janet's church campaign; however, it showed the ineptness of editor Clara.

Janet once had accommodated the request of neighbor Maddie Fitzsimmons to take a photo of Maddie's Cub Scout troop touring the local zoo. Janet submitted the picture to Clara, who put it on the front page; not only did the photo look out of place, but it featured one of Clara's headline gems: "Cubs Visited Zoo."

As Kitty remarked upon seeing that edition: "I'd get fired from the copydesk at The Trib if I wrote that headline. You don't write heads in the past tense, and besides, cubs LIVE at the darn zoo."

On this bright morning, Janet and Clara exchanged their usual niceties, which always included an inquiry from Clara: "How do you do it, Janet? With the children and your column in the Hartford Tribune and everything else."

"Drink. That is the secret, Clara. Keep chuggin' them down and you don't notice the kids."

Clara lacked a sense of humor. She took everything seriously, it seemed to Janet and the rest of Dunfield.

"You really drink, Janet?"

"Only kidding. You know I am a pillar of St. Matthew's Church."

Clara seemed as if she did not even understand the conversation, so Janet switched subjects quickly.

"What's new here at The Call, Clara? Same old routine?"

"Not for long, it appears."

Clara proceeded to detail the impending sale of The Dunfield Call, owned by 85-year-old millionaire Mildred Rockwell, widow of the original publisher, Gilbert Rockwell.

Mr. Rockwell had inherited millions from his gentleman-farming family. He dabbled in several businesses, but his love was The Call because it seemed to give him a certain power in the region.

The Dunfield Call debuted in the 1950s and it became the weekly reading fare of residents in several towns west of Hartford. The paper had no reporters, per se; the editor infrequently covered some local commissions and municipal court sessions. Ad rates were low; The Call attracted only local advertisers while national companies flocked to the daily Hartford Tribune's display pages.

Mr. Rockwell had never cared about making much money on his newspaper venture; the 8,000-circulation paper proved more of a hobby to the millionaire. His wife spent her spare time on shopping sprees in Boston and Manhattan. Her lack of interest in The Dunfield Call continued after her spouse's death. She put the paper in the hands of a Hartford lawyer, Jack Mason, who in turn relied on Clara to handle everything on the editorial side. Mrs.

Rockwell would check in periodically from her Palm Beach jet-set life or her Cape Cod summer home; she never bothered to visit the paper's offices on Dunfield's Main Street.

This sale could mark the end of my publicity days, smiled the sarcastic Janet to herself. If The Call were purchased by a credible newspaper group, it might be more difficult to get the church publicity on the front page. She knew full well, though, that a respected news firm would lack interest in a buying a news-less and profitless Dunfield Call.

"They want more than a million for it," Clara continued.

"For this rag?" Janet remarked before realizing what she said to the editor.

Clara appeared puzzled...and irritated.

"Uh, rag, you know, Clara. That's a slang word for paper. During the Revolutionary War, rags were used to make paper. In fact, as part of the war effort, colonial women would save old rags to be made into paper."

"Maybe you'd like to buy this rag," Clara responded in what seemed to be a bit of an abrasive tone.

"I wouldn't pay a million dollars if I had it. I wouldn't pay a quarter of a million. Hey, I'm not in that bracket. I'm in the quarter-pounder category these days."

With that, she turned, walked out to Main Street, took out her cell phone, and phoned Kitty.

"Meet me at McDonald's. You won't believe what I have to tell you."

CHAPTER 6

RICK AND MADELINE CARTER RESIDED in Dunfield's contribution to American history---a structure that had housed colonial troops during the siege of Dunfield. Most Americans to this day are unfamiliar with that bit of 1770s lore when eight enlisted men from General George Washington's Valley Forge unit had become disillusioned with the war and the weather. Unlike their fellow soldiers who were inspired by Thomas Paine's writings and geared for victory at Trenton, these eight Massachusetts residents never listened to more than Paine's introductory words: "These are the times that try men's souls."

The eight agreed that their souls had been tried and they were tired, so they quietly exited the ghastly Valley Force camp scene and headed back to their New England roots.

Days later, after a march they never could describe, they found themselves in Dunfield, Ct., west of Hartford. They celebrated their freedom by downing brew after brew, courtesy of other patrons, and describing their made-up battlefield bravery to those at the famed Dunfield Pub. When these self-proclaimed war heroes emerged from their drunken stupor into the cold but sunny Main Street of Dunfield, they suddenly reverted to their battle mentality. Within hours, the lovely homes that dotted Main Street resembled the aftermath of a typhoon. Throwing stones, the soldiers broke windows; they stripped properties of winter foliage, and even bedecked some homes with multi-colored paints taken from the town hardware store.

This blight on the town's history has been termed "The Siege of Dunfield." After the three-hour war game ended, the eight soldiers dropped to their sleep on the front yard of the residence of Hunter Carter, a banker who lived in what was considered the finest residence in the area. Upon his arrival home that day, Carter found his domestic staff attending to the needs of the servicemen camped out on his lawn. He had no idea they were deserters. Carter, who had contributed many dollars to the anti-British efforts, considered these men as heroes because he had heard about their self-reported tales of victory. He offered not only to house the group, but to pay for the damages incurred in their drunken rampage.

Throughout the next few days, the soldiers enjoyed the hospitality and amenities of the Carter household. Then a uniformed duo from Washington's staff arrived in Dunfield in search of the AWOL 8. Carter realized he had been taken by a bunch of hustlers, so he quietly instituted his own war game. Early the following morning, he roused the unknowing soldiers from bed and ordered them out of his house.

"Just give us our clothes," begged one young soldier, who like his colleagues, slept in the buff under the warm covers on the Carter beds.

"Sorry," answered Carter.

So, as the story goes, the eight who arrived as Revolutionary heroes now marched naked up Main Street to the stares of townspeople.

That tale of the 18th Century romp of Washington's soldiers always surfaced when Rick and Madeline Carter hosted their annual spring cocktail party on the lawn of the historic family home that had been willed to them.

Janet Watson, immersed in conversation with a group of other party guests, suggested laughingly that the Carters should recreate the soldiers' bash as a tribute to the town's history.

"I'll think about it," chuckled Rick, "but who wants to bare the brunt of the laughs?"

The idea of re-staging the "Siege of Dunfield" became a main topic of conversation at the party and, at one point, while a large group was gathered, Janet remarked quite loudly to her friend Kitty McIntyre: "We'll cover it. In fact, let's push for it in an editorial."

Others in the group appeared puzzled by the conversation.

"And where will you print it?" asked Martha Rainey, whose name and loudmouthed reputation had earned her the nickname Martha Raye.

"We're buying The Dunfield Call," answered Kitty with a smirk on her face.

The conversation stopped. Partygoers stared at Kitty and Janet.

Frank McDow, a Dunfield town councilman in his early 50s, marched to the spot where Janet and Kitty had shocked the assemblage.

"You're not really buying the paper, are you? You two?"

"You are looking at The Call Girls," beamed Kitty's spouse, Dr. Tim McIntyre, smiling at the elected official whose construction business reportedly flourished on work issued by the town. Tim disliked McDow from the time a decade ago when the latter fired Tim's dad, Mike, a veteran McDow foreman who tried to blow the whistle on what he considered unfair labor practices. Mike died a few months later of what Tim called a "broken heart."

"Who's putting up the money?" asked McDow as he looked at Hank Watson.

The McIntyres and Watsons just smiled in concert at McDow.

But they said nothing. Janet merely opened her purse, took out a pad, and began taking notes. News of the impending change of ownership swept through the lawn party and guests flocked to Janet and Kitty to ask about their plans for the paper.

"We are going to cover everything," remarked Janet as she eyed the hapless McDow.

"This is a calm, historic town," said McDow as if he already feared a new, journalistic Siege of Dunfield with the two women at the helm of the paper-of-record.

"Journalists write the first draft of history," smiled Kitty. "The Call will soon be as famous as this historic lawn."

CHAPTER 7

———

KITTY MCINTYRE PACED BACK AND forth across the plush carpeting at the offices of Mason and Smith, attorneys-at-law. Her mind raced from 5-year-old Timmy, whom she had just dropped off at mini-soccer camp, to the beaches at Chatham on the Cape, where she had spent the previous week, to the property closing about to take place.

"Power and poverty," she mumbled aloud.

"What?" inquired Tim, who delayed his Wednesday tee-off time to participate in the transaction that would net him a newspaper---or at least a quarter of it.

"We're about to assume journalistic power while going into the poorhouse," answered Kitty, as she continued to strut across the green rug.

She became annoyed by her own pacing.

"Tim, did you do this pacing when you were waiting for Timmy's birth?"

"I was IN the delivery room, Kits---are you losing your mind? I was doing the damn breathing stuff with you."

"How could I forget that?" laughed Kitty, recalling how dentist Tim kept comparing the use of forceps to the procedure for re-moving a tooth. The obstetrician, obviously annoyed by the verbal intrusion into the delivery process, finally screamed: "Thank God you're not a taxidermist."

Kitty's thought patterns were interrupted by the entrance of Hank and Janet Watson into the legal suite.

And some entrance it was---Janet, wearing a neck brace; Hank, holding the year- old twins, Bret and Billy, and 4-year-old Marta and 2 1/2-year old Molly, tagging behind the crew.

"Don't ask," commented Janet, looking as if she had been drained of the final bit of energy needed to sustain the mother of four preschoolers.

Hank began to elaborate on the activities of the previous evening.

"Everything was going well," he said in his sarcastic but humorous tone. "All the troops had been fed and bathed and were nestled all snug in their beds. Janet and I sat down to a gourmet repast, featuring Pinot Noir and lo mein---you can't beat China Express takeout---when all of a sudden, there arose such a clatter."

The noise, he said, emanated from a bedroom shared by Marta and Molly.

"I trudged upstairs," said Hank, "and went into the room where I found two little girls laughing and having the time of their lives. Seems they snuck out of bed and took lipstick from their mother's dresser. Then they proceeded to use it on their faces, their legs, their clothes, their beds... it was a Revlon phenomenon. So I took away the weapons of their rampage, went to the top of the steps, and in a controlled voice, yelled to Janet: 'These daughters of yours just lipsticked the whole goddam place.' Janet tore upstairs, into the girls' room and then disappeared into the hardwood floor with a thump that made the house rock. She had tripped over Elsa Marie."

"Who?" inquired Tim.

"One of those friggin' Cabbage Patch dolls that have names... Elsa Marie...Amanda Susanna...Ramona Alicia...they were the rage in the early '80s. Our neighbor gave the kids her collection of them."

"God, this neck hurts," moaned Janet as the twins started crying at the same time that Attorney Jack Mason entered the room.

"Jack, I'll tell you briefly and believe it," said Hank. "Janet tripped over Elsa Marie after Marta and Molly lipsticked themselves. I took Janet to the emergency room while our neighbor, Marion Foley, and her daughter Elsa---isn't that ironic?---watched and washed the kids. Janet has some jarring in her neck and has to wear that contraption which costs $250 at St. Mark's Hospital where the overweight head nurse in the ER is worth a story herself. Janet couldn't sleep all night because of the pain. Then we find out that Mrs. Crane, who was to babysit this morning, is ill---probably at the thought of watching the Watson gang---so here we are with the offspring in tow to buy The Dunfield Call."

Kitty's journalistic mind evaded any comment of sympathy.

"Janet, I'm glad you're going to keep your 'Oh, Mother' column in the Tribune. You've got your topic of the week."

"Kitty, how can I help run The Call? I have four kiddies, a sprained neck, no babysitter, a Tribune column to write, a house that looks like a barracks, and now I'm going to be an entrepreneur? I'm weak."

Into the room at this chaotic moment strolled a distinguished elderly woman.

"Do you babysit?" asked Tim sort of casually.

The lady frowned at the ill-timed remark.

"I want you to meet Mrs. Rockwell," stated Mason in his deepest courtroom voice.

Janet eyed Kitty, who was throwing dagger stares at her spouse and his attempt at humor. Mrs. Rockwell was no babysitter, except perhaps for a poodle or bilingual parrot. She was the owner---lock, stock and barrel---of The Dunfield Call, and had journeyed from her Hyannis summer residence to attend the proceedings. Mason had told the owners-to-be that Mrs. Rockwell would not appear, and that the necessary papers would be pre-signed by her.

Now the dowager faced the pride and joy of the parenting club; it was a scene out of an Erma Bombeck column.

"Are you the women who want to buy The Call?"

"Yes," answered Janet and Kitty in unison.

A young secretary entered the room and offered to take the Watson children to a nearby playground. She explained that she already had called her teenage sister to assist in this act of mercy.

Mason, who obviously had assigned this task to his employee, said "Great!"

As the screaming Watson quartet exited, Mrs. Rockwell inquired: "Where are you getting the financing?"

Hank explained: "We are buying this together. Tim, a dentist, and his wife Kitty, a seasoned copy editor. Yours truly---I'm a VP at Hartford Bank, and my wife, Janet, a former sportswriter and now a Hartford Tribune columnist. We have a loan of $200,000 from my father-in-law, and the four of us added $400,000 of our own funds, mostly from selling stock we owned. We arranged a mortgage from my bank for the rest, and we think we can cover a lot of the mortgage from income and from rental of the apartments over The Call offices. We have signed statements from Dr. Denis, my father-in-law, that if we run short initially, he will help us cover the costs."

"Can you keep The Call as respectable as it has been?" asked Mrs. Rockwell.

Janet groaned. She wanted to laugh but fortunately her outburst made it appear as if her ailing neck had been hit by a sharp pain. All she could think was how funny it was that Mrs. Rockwell would consider The Call a respectable publication. The Palm Beach matron obviously was unaware of how Dunfielders referred to it as "Don't Call It a Paper."

Kitty looked a bit tired herself as she mulled the comments of the millionaire widow. It was a look Janet had seen before on the face of her would-be partner.

"I'm getting cold feet," she had said to Janet two days earlier as the pair discussed the venture.

"Maybe if you take your toes out of the kiddie pool you won't have such cold feet," retorted Janet.

The two women had been sandwiched among hundreds on a 100-degree day at The Dunfield Community Pool. Timmy, Marta and Molly were jumping up and down in the water while their mothers took guard duty on the wall beside the foot-high pool.

Apparently the cocktail party revelation about the impending purchase of The Call had weaved its way among the young Dunfield mothers. From the time Janet and Kitty entered the pool area, inquiring females repeatedly had smirked: "You're not really buying the paper?"

Janet, happy to have a break from the home front, where a vacationing Hank was watching the twins, let the remarks fly by without responding. Kitty had taken a defensive position, acknowledging the upcoming purchase and assuring the skeptical women that "things will change."

Now, in Jack Mason's legal offices, Kitty continued to be defensive in answer to Mrs. Rockwell's inquiry about continuing to publish a respectable publication.

"The Call has been a special part of this town, and will continue to be," Kitty blurted out.

Janet's neck was getting worse, probably because she had to keep turning away to avoid getting hysterical with laughter. She agreed silently that The Call always would be part of the town but she was yearning to say to Mrs. Rockwell: "What is special about the paper is that we are buying it."

The sound of the Watson children at the nearby playground reverberated through the law offices as Jack Mason completed the paperwork and all parties signed on the respective lines.

Janet looked at Kitty as if to say "We did it. This crazy pair of newswomen turned-homemakers/moms now owns The Dunfield Call." But she uttered no words except "Thanks" as congratulations poured forth from the group.

On the way out, Kitty remarked to her friend: "Janet, we are sticking our necks out this time."

The suffering Janet looked up from her neck brace and responded: "Funny, Kitty. And I thought I was the comedic one in this duo!"

The Call Girls were on their way to local notoriety.

CHAPTER 8

———

THE TOUGHEST DECISION FACED BY the new Call owners regarded the employment of Clara Woodruff. The oversized, dowdy spinster had been at the helm of The Call since Gilbert Rockwell hired her in the 1990s. Clara lacked basic journalistic skills and published anything sent in by local church groups, real estate firms or mothers of brides. The headlines were usually "split," a mortal sin in the news business, and thus drew the wrath of new co-owner Kitty McIntyre, the award-winning copy editor.

Sometimes Clara's headlines represented Freudian slips. Kitty's collections of "Bad Heads" included one published several years previously in The Dunfield Call; the headline, printed on a story about the appointment of a woman principal at Dunfield Middle School, read "Woman Takes Top Position."

"I'd say that was a bit Freudian," Kitty told her friends.

Clara could not determine even the slightest faux pas in the scores of press releases that arrived daily at The Call. She once printed, apparently straight from a college release, that "Next semester, Michael Walters will head for Europe on a fellowship." Kitty cut out the article for her files with a note: "Is he going on a Cunard liner?"

But Clara's lack of journalistic knowledge was offset by her organizational talent and her interaction with people. She was well-liked and a hard worker.

"She has never covered Town Council," screamed Kitty at an informal organizing meeting with Janet a few weeks before they took over the paper's reins.

"It's her bread and butter," argued Janet. "She is in her late 50s. Not married. She needs a job. How would you like to be bounced out at that age and have no income?"

"OK. Damn it. We'll train her," said Kitty. "Heck, she is a graduate of Smith College but God knows what she studied there. You handle the reporting, Jan, and I will work with her on editing and layout. And she can keep us apprised at all times about everything going on at The Call when we are not there."

So the stage was set. Janet and Kitty agreed that their families came first and that neither would spend more than two full days in the office. Janet came in on Mondays, when most of the copy arrived, and on Wednesday, when production was in full swing. Kitty worked Tuesdays to edit copy and to help with the layout on the computer system, and she joined Janet on Wednesdays to double-check the editions that were printed at a local firm that afternoon for Thursday arrival by local mail. Clara put in a five-day week under her new title, managing editor. They carried cell phones to be in touch at all times.

Janet and Kitty shared the titles of editors/publishers, although those terms meant little in terms of work division. They handled editorial duties, business, and production, depending on the day of the week. Direct phone lines, computers and FAX machines in their homes made access to the paper quite easy and allowed them to work from their kitchens when they so chose. They decided that an online edition would be needed but not until the regular issues were up and running smoothly.

The babysitter problems were ironed out easily. A number of grandmother-type women responded to an advertised job to "split duties with two families." In the end, the publishers hired a robust 55-year-old practical nurse, Ann Wilson, who split her time as a nanny between the two households. Janet dubbed her "Nanny Annie" and the name stuck.

The streamer headline on the first edition of the under-new-ownership paper read: **"Local Residents Purchase The Call."**

The accompanying article spotlighted the background of the new editors/publishers:

> *Kitty Moran McIntyre, an alumna of St. Agnes Academy, Hartford, received her AB in journalism from Syracuse University and her MA in English from the University of Connecticut. She served four years on the international copy desk of the Washington Post before joining the Hartford Tribune as a copy editor. She and her husband, Dr. Timothy McIntyre, are Dunfield natives. They reside with their son, Timmy, on Birch Road.*
>
> *Janet Denis Watson, also a Dunfield native and St. Agnes graduate, received her bachelor's degree from the University of Missouri School of Journalism and a master's in communications from Boston University. She is a former sportswriter for The Philadelphia Inquirer and The Hartford Tribune, and writes a weekly column, "Oh, Mother," for the Tribune. She and her husband, Henry J., reside on Fuller Brook Road with their four children: Marta, Molly, Bret and Billy.*

The lead article also detailed the history of The Call, from its birth in the 1950s to its most recent change in ownership. Even the $1.8

million purchase price---for the business and the building--- was revealed.

"We have to put it in," Kitty had argued, "because we are going to begin publishing all of the real estate transactions in the area. They are public record."

Yes, that was among the changes to be made under the new regime. In a sidebar to the main story, Kitty and Janet listed a number of other planned changes, including regular coverage of town meetings, a stronger editorial page, details of municipal court cases, and a column penned by the new publishers.

And there, smack in the middle of the front page of the new Dunfield Call, was a three-column photo of Kitty McIntyre and Janet Watson at work in their new offices.

The posed picture, as Kitty had said, "will never match the last photo of us in The Dunfield Call."

Seventeen years earlier, Kitty and Janet has been the subject of a Dunfield Call article about the annual St. Agnes Academy canoe race. The front- page photo featured the pair, then high school seniors, paddling to victory under a sign reading "The Finish Line." Tall, lanky, blonde Kitty sat in the canoe with her long arms outstretched and her head bent forward as if she were giving it her all for the final push to the win. Behind her in the canoe sat Janet, her dark hair under a baseball cap and her mouth clenched as she paddled to the finish line.

The picture's focus, as Sister Margaret Anne so delicately put it to the girls later, was not the excitement on the two students' faces, but the fact that each was sporting a two-piece bathing suit and both had cigarettes extending from their mouths.

Underneath the picture ran a 15-inch story. In part it read:

The annual St. Agnes Academy event, which draws entries from throughout the student body, is designed to foster a competitive spirit within a fun-filled atmosphere.

The Misses Denis and Moran, seniors and both Dunfield residents, have teamed together for four years and twice copped runnerup honors before taking first place in this year's competition. For Miss Denis, the win was sweet because, she said, "it was our last chance to compete." Miss Moran called the victory "a test of our abilities."

But the real test of their abilities---to remain at St. Agnes---came several days after the article was published in The Call. That's how long it took for the word to travel from Mrs. Wadsworth Ellis, an octogenarian Dunfield resident and St. Agnes alumna, back to Sister Margaret Anne, the 6-foot, 240-pound school directress in her late 60s. Mrs. Ellis reportedly phoned Sister Margaret Anne to ask why the school would allow cigarette-smoking, swimsuit-clad ladies in a canoe race.

Initially, the nun ignored the concerns and blamed the call on Mrs. Ellis's path to senility. But when another stalwart graduate actually mailed The Call's front page to her, Sister Margaret Anne, according to her secretary, almost tore her hair out. And, as Janet later remarked: 'That is no easy feat for a nun in a starched habit."

Meanwhile, Kitty and Janet were the talk of the St. Agnes cafeteria, where The Call had been passed from table to table during the week.

"We pulled it off," laughed Kitty to her fellow seniors one noontime. "The paper actually published a story about a race that never happened. My mother is furious."

"My mother hasn't mentioned it," added Janet. "But then she hasn't spoken to me since. I'm not allowed at the dinner table. I heard her tell my father that she sent me to that Catholic school so I would learn to behave like a perfect young woman."

When the boom fell, it came quickly. Sister Margaret Anne didn't wait to call the duo to her office. The jumbo-sized administrator stormed into the cafeteria and, with the front page of The Call in her hands, hustled right over to Kitty and Janet and said: "Spare me, O Lord, as I deal with this bunch of truck."

The entire cafeteria assemblage got hysterical. They thought Sister Margaret Anne had said something that rhymed with "truck."

Janet turned to Kitty: "I think we are in trouble."

Now, 17 years after the incident, and as they put their first edition of The Dunfield Call "to bed," Janet and Kitty recounted the days that followed the "March of Sister Margaret Anne" into the St. Agnes Academy lunchroom.

"I remember how she grabbed your hair, Kitty, and then pulled you from your seat," laughed Janet. "I was on the other end of the table and Louise Loftus, who was sitting next to me, kept whispering 'Don't mention my name.' Then we were whisked out of the room."

"To the cheers of the entire student body," chuckled Kitty.

She got a bit emotional as she recalled how her mother reacted when the parents were ordered to report to the academy's main office.

"Here she was, president of the Mothers' Club and she had to face Sister Margaret Anne."

"Thank God she was the president of the Mothers' Club, Kitty, or we'd have our diplomas from Dunfield High."

"Why'd we do that anyway?" asked Kitty, still apparently thinking about her mother. Mary Moran, a County Mayo native whose beauty was matched by her lovable personality, had been killed in an auto accident shortly after Kitty entered Syracuse University.

"It was your idea, Kitty," responded Janet. "You wanted to prove to Sister St. John, that idea of a journalism teacher, that Connecticut weeklies published anything that was sent in if it looked real."

"Well, it did look real, Janet. Your article was a polished press release, and that picture of us---how did we ever talk sweet Louise Loftus into coming down to Wethersfield to take that? Remember how she put up 'The Finish Line' sign? And to think she became a nun!"

The new editors/publishers spent more than an hour recounting the fabricated story, their two months cleaning brass in the chapel, and their mothers' promise to Sister Margaret Anne to run a card party/fashion show to raise funds for the school library. Kitty and Janet still saluted themselves for convincing Sister Margaret Anne NOT to write a letter to the editor of The Call because, as they told her, "that would hurt St. Agnes Academy's reputation even more."

"And she listened to us---can you believe it?" asked Janet. "To this day Dunfield Call readers think St. Agnes Academy actually has an annual canoe race and that we won it in our senior year."

"That's it, Jan---you are a petite brunette genius even to this day," said Kitty.

"What do you mean?"

"We're having trouble trying to figure out what to call the column we are going to write in The Call, correct?"

"Right."

"How about something referring to our first picture in this paper 17 years ago?"

"Why not," said Janet, who was game for anything.

And thus was launched the pair's weekly column: "The Finish Line."

CHAPTER 9

———

WHEN JANET WATSON STROLLED INTO the meeting of the Dunfield Recreation Commission, Chairman Jim Dodd looked up in surprise.

"What are you doing here?" he inquired of the tired-looking Janet, who had finished dressing the offspring quartet for bed before kissing Hank goodbye."

"I'm here to cover the meeting."

No one outside the six appointed commissioners and Richard Ross, the town's recreation director, ever attended these evening sessions, so the presence of one of the new Call owners made Janet's appearance quite formidable.

Earlier that day, she had obtained a copy of the agenda at Town Hall, and noticed Ross was to update the commission on the staffing of the town pool and summer playgrounds, which had been operating for about several weeks. The appointments piqued Janet's interest after she heard Faith Sullivan, the wife of Mayor Kevin Sullivan, tell friends at the pool one day that her son Kurt was working as a lifeguard there and her daughter Mindy was a counselor at Madison School playground.

The Recreation Commission meeting started with a discussion of new tennis courts in town. Then Ross, the recreation director, began his report on the summer staffers.

Dodd, the commission head, interrupted.

"You don't have to do that, Mr. Ross---everything is going well at the pool and the playground."

Ross responded: "I have a list of the summer employees if anyone wants them."

Then Ed Brown, a retired physical education teacher and veteran Rec Commission member, argued: "Read the names, Jim. They're right in front of you."

Janet noticed that Ed Brown was smirking as chairman Dodd uncomfortably started to read from the list. The pool/playground staff included collegians with last names like Sullivan, Waters, Haynes, Evans. Their fathers were Recreation Commission members or town politicos. Janet recognized at least five other names of staffers whose parents were active on town commissions.

At the end of the session, Janet asked Dodd for a printed list of the appointees.

"You heard the names I read," he answered in a nasty voice.

"I want a copy," she said. "I have a right to that information under the Public Access law. Besides, you did not give the name of the pool supervisor."

Ed Brown walked over to Janet and handed over his own copy. She searched quickly for the information she sought. Pool director: James Dodd Jr.

She looked at Dodd and asked: "Why didn't you mention that your son was named to the highest-paid summer post?"

Chairman Dodd turned and exited the meeting room without answering the question.

Ed Brown turned to Janet: "I look forward to reading The Call this week."

While working alone the next day, Kitty edited Janet's piece on the Recreation Commission session. She smiled as she read the lead:

James Dodd Jr., son of the chairman of Dunfield's Recreation Commission, has been named pool director this year, and children of other commissioners and town officials also are serving on the pool and playground staffs. The elder Dodd failed to mention his own son's name as he read the list of summer appointees during a Recreation Commission meeting Monday night. Dodd also refused to comment on why his son was appointed to the highest-paying summer job.

Kitty read the entire article without changing a word.

"What a story," she remarked to Clara, who was opening the mail at the next desk. Kitty then wrote the front-page headline: **Dodd's Son Heads Pool Staff**. The kicker, over the main head, said: **Rec Commissioners Appoint Own Offspring**

Janet also had penned a "Finish Line" column about her attendance at the Recreation Commission meeting, noting that Dodd appeared shocked at her arrival and detailing his refusal to answer questions.

Kitty phoned Janet, who was ensconced in her basement family room where she was watching Sesame Street reruns with the kids while she folded the wash.

"Thank God for Pampers," said Janet as she answered the direct line from The Call.

"Don't say that too loudly, Jan. Some of our advertisers are environmental advocates, I assume. Called to tell you I just read your Rec Commission story and the column---both pieces are super. Don't you think we also should hit them with an editorial about access to public records?"

"Yeah, go ahead and write one. And send Clara over to Town Hall to get the resumes of the pool and playground staffers. I have a feeling we might find some interesting data."

"OK, Janet, will do. Talk to you later. Enjoy the Mommy track today."

Only 30 days after its purchase, The Call was in full swing. Already Clara Woodruff was adapting to her new role, in which she actually helped assemble information while continuing to select and edit incoming material. Kitty and Janet worked together---or alone---as their schedules dictated.

Iris Drozic, a pleasant woman in her mid-40s, joined the staff as part-time receptionist and circulation director. And Ken Masterson busily devoted more than 40 hours a week to selling ads for The Call.

Masterson was a 26-year-old UConn graduate. At 6 feet, 7 inches tall, the bespectacled advertising manager stood out in the newsroom crowd. He had joined The Call a year earlier in the Rockwell era after spending two years as an ad salesman at a Massachusetts paper. Ken was organized and he was good---ad sales, while still not up to par in the estimation of the new owners, had increased 15 percent since his arrival at the paper.

As she penned an editorial about public records access, Kitty heard Clara say "Whoa---take a look at this letter that I just opened."

She handed a piece of fancy stationery to Kitty, who read the letter out loud.

Dear Editor:

My daughter Muffy's wedding story was published in your paper last week. I wrote the account myself, with all the details about what the wedding party wore and the decorations in the church. I was so upset when I read the article because you took out all that marvelous information about my daughter's beautiful dress and the topiary trees that lined the aisles. I could not believe it. The Dunfield

Call always put in that lovely information for its readers. If this is what the new owners think about a social page, then you can cancel my subscription. And I hope my friends will follow suit.

Mrs. Herbert P. White III

"Christ," mumbled Kitty. "I figured we'd have some trouble there. We are going to have to explain our new wedding article policy in a two-column, 10-point boldface box this week."

"People are going to have fits," said Clara.

"For awhile. But I am also announcing a policy change that will be well-received by lots of people. No longer will we restrict the pictures to brides only; we'll publish pictures of the couple, even if they're gay."

"Wow," said Clara, "you are forging into new journalistic territory in this blueblood area."

"No, I'm not, Clara," said Kitty. "I'm simply satisfying my own curiosity. Wouldn't you like to see what kind of a jerk married Muffy White?"

CHAPTER 10

KEN MASTERSON LOOKED LIKE A lighthouse---tall and pale---as he entered The Call offices. Janet and Kitty, both checking the copy before it was transferred electronically to a printer in Rocky Hill, inquired about his dazed look.

"Haynes pulled his advertising."

Larry Haynes owned the drugstore that abutted The Call's building. He had inherited the building from his father and had continued to book weekly ads about the store's specials on everything from cosmetics to candies.

"He gave it to me in spades," said Ken, detailing how Haynes referred to the paper as a "yellow journalism rag."

"Can we quote him on that?" asked Janet.

"Go over and interview him, Jan. We have nothing to lose. We already lost his $200-a-week ad," said Kitty.

Janet swapped loafers for heels, donned a linen jacket to match her slacks, and in professional sartorial splendor, walked into Haynes Drugs.

At Janet's request, a counter saleswoman headed for the back office to get Mr. Haynes.

The pot-bellied, bald Haynes, who could pass for Kojak in golf togs, briskly approached Janet and said: "You want to see me?"

"Yes," answered Janet. "I'm following up on a Recreation Commission appointments story, which I am sure you saw last week in our paper, by talking to you and other commissioners. I also want to respond to your comments to our advertising manager that our paper is a yellow journalism rag."

"That paper is a goddam piece of crap," he said. "Are you trying to ruin this town?

Janet insisted: "Why did you call it yellow journalism, Mr. Haynes?"

"Because that is what you are making it—a sensational rag."

He seemed a bit intimidated as Janet jotted notes in her reporter's notepad. "Can you tell me what constitutes yellow journalism, Mr. Haynes?"

"Dammit, don't you know?"

"As a matter of fact, I do," smiled Janet, who earned an A in a tough journalism history class at Mizzou. "In the late 19th Century yellow journalism surfaced in New York courtesy of a cartoon called The Yellow Kid..."

"Who cares?' interrupted Haynes. "We'll ruin you before you ruin us."

Using a reportorial technique, Janet repeated the phrase loudly as she wrote it down: "We'll ruin you before you ruin us." This was one quote that would make the next edition of The Call. Janet reached into her pocket and pulled out a piece of paper. It was a copy of the application of Haynes' son Leonard for a lifeguard job at the town pool. The copy had been obtained at Town Hall by Clara Woodruff, whose former reluctance to engage in true journalistic work had turned to a sense of accomplishment that she had argued for her right to see public information.

"Mr. Haynes, the application does not mention when your son passed the Red Cross lifesaving tests. Can you fill me in?"

"Where the hell did you get that application? You can't get records like that."

"I am not going to list the laws that give people access to this information---Mr. Haynes, when did your son pass the required lifesaving tests?"

"Get the hell out of here," ordered Haynes as Janet continued to add to her notes. "I'll never advertise in your rag."

"But you'll get your name in it for free," she stated.

Janet rushed to The Call offices and yelled: "Stop the presses."

That was an old term used in newsrooms when papers were typeset in the backshop and then taken in plates for printing. But now the paper was designed on computers and sent electronically to the printer, who ran off copies. At The Call, most papers were delivered through the mail, so the printer had to make sure the copies got to the Post Office in time to get them to subscribers' homes on the following day.

To accommodate the new story on Haynes, some of the stories on the front page had to be moved to inside pages.

"We have to send these pages to the printer in about a half-hour," said Kitty.

"Send the inside pages and ask for another half-hour for the front page. We will pay the over-costs to the printer," said Janet.

"What did Haynes have to say?"

"That we would be ruined."

"That fat, bald Rec Commissioner said that?" screamed Kitty as she picked up the phone to call Newsome Printing and make arrangements for the delayed schedule. "Make sure you put in that quote."

"Yahoo, this is what a town paper is all about," laughed Janet as she started typing on her computer. "Good, hard investigative work that takes your mind off everything else, including the kids!"

Halfway through her speedwriting chores she received a phone call from Nanny Annie.

"I think Marta has the measles."

Janet quickly finished the story, put on her loafers and grabbed her car keys. As she headed for the door, she turned to her Call colleagues: "Looks as if I am on my way to a **spot** news story."

Kitty sighed: "She will never change, gang, but her copy is great."

CHAPTER 11

———

SEPTEMBER HIT LIKE A BOMBSHELL as it always does at weekly newspapers. The summer dearth of press releases, meeting notices
and news in general had given away to an avalanche of mail and
e-mail messages that offered information about everything from
Girl Scout sign-ups to school lunch menus. Clara spent half
the morning just checking e-mail or accepting hand-delivered
releases.

For Kitty, tanned after a week at The Vineyard, and for Janet,
who had survived Marta and Molly's measles and the twins' snif-
fles, the fall was destined to be a hectic period. For one thing, the
regular monthly meetings of the Town Council, the School Board
and other town bodies were about to resume.

Only the Recreation Commission met regularly in the summer, and The Call's coverage of that group was becoming legion.
Haynes had convinced only one other merchant, a men's store pro-
prietor, to drop his advertising in The Call. The volume of letters-
to-the-editors, most expressing disgust at the summer political
appointments, had filled the pages of the papers for several weeks.

"The Finish Line" proved welcome copy at the home of the paper's 10,000 subscribers. The column was timely, well-written, and
often displayed the humorous pen of its co-author, Janet Watson.

Her column about the "Pooper Scooper Law" exemplified Janet's talent for writing. She got disgusted one day when Molly stepped in "dog dirt" at the Wilson Middle School playground, which had become the regular morning destination for people walking their dogs. Janet had read a few years previously that the town had enacted a Pooper Scooper law mandating that dog owners had to clean up after their canines. The messes at the Wilson School playground were proof, she believed, that the town never enforced the legislation.

So, after a bit of checking about the town law and with the support of her co-writer, Kitty, she took to the power of the pen. In part, the column read:

> *The Pooper Scooper Law is not for the dogs.*
> *It's for the birds.*
> *Three years on the books, and never once has it been enforced! That might be fine for the dogs, but it's unfair to the mother who has to de-poop her child's sneakers and to residents in general.*
> *Just the other day, I watched as a nicely-dressed man, walking a rather ugly mongrel, passed by my Fuller Brook Road abode. The doggie "went" right on my lawn.*
> *So I went right out the door.*
> *"Do you know there's a Pooper Scooper law in Dunfield?" I asked. He responded with a four-letter word that, ironically, described what his dog had just done on the lawn!*

"The Finish Line" column proceeded to spell out the law. Janet questioned why it never had been enforced and even quoted Police Chief Stephen Hazelle that "we don't have time to deal with it."

Then Janet, in her witty vein, finished the column with her own solution to the dog-pooping problem.

I am so mad that I've made a two-line sign that hangs over our big elm tree near the sidewalk. The sign reads:
HOW DO YOU SPELL RELIEF?
N-O-T H-E-R-E.

The day after that "Finish Line" column appeared in an August edition of The Call, the owner of a local art/frame shop walked into the paper's offices.

"I am so sick of dogs on my lawn. I just loved that column, so I framed it for you. Hope you don't mind."

"Mind?" said Kitty, who had been fielding calls praising her partner. "Janet will love it."

Kitty turned and hung the framed column on the wall space she had reserved for "future awards."

"This is an award, in my book," she told the other Call staffers as the art shop owner left.

"It's a shock, I'd say," mumbled Ken Masterson. "I tried three times last year to get that art shop lady to buy ads and she always said: "Who reads that paper?""

CHAPTER 12

—

JANET WISHED SHE HAD BROUGHT along some cotton swabs to Marta's first day in prekindergarten.

Hand-in-hand, mother and child walked the four blocks to Madison School in the company of neighbors Holly Kramer and her son Charlie.

Marta was about to begin pre-kindergarten, a special program for 4- and 5-year-olds. Operated by the school district, the pre-kindergarten classes were not free: parents who wished to enroll their children paid $300 a month for the privilege.

"It's cheaper than nursery school," Janet told Hank. "And the kids do many things with the regular kindergarten class."

The auburn-haired Marta looked angelic in her blue corduroy dress, replete with a simple lace collar. All of the first-day students appeared well-groomed in their new togs as Mrs. Prince, the head pre-kindergarten teacher, addressed the crowd on a grassy knoll outside the school building.

Janet kept leaning ahead to hear what Mrs. Prince was saying. She was not sure if the woman was issuing rules about "wearing boots" on rainy days or maybe she was discussing "snack fruits."

"I wish I had some Q-tips," Janet whispered to Holly. "Think I should clean my ears."

"Janet," said Holly, "I don't think even the kids can hear the whispers of that woman."

As Janet and Holly walked back home, the latter shook her head and commented: "I do not know why they let that woman teach pre-kindergarten."

"That bad?" answered Janet. "I know she can't yell at the kids--- all she seems to do is whisper."

Holly proceeded to enlighten Janet about the pre-K experiences of her older two children.

"One day Mrs. Prince lost her shoes. She had worn good shoes to school and switched to bedroom slippers, which she always puts on in class, from what the kids say. Then, in the afternoon, she told the children she could not find her shoes. So, while she sat at the desk and cried, the whole bunch of little kiddies had a treasure hunt for Mrs. Prince's shoes. Know where they were?"

"Where?"

"On her feet! She apparently forgot she had changed at noon-time when she went out to lunch with some of the other teachers."

Holly continued: "I didn't believe Tommy when he told me that, but all the kids told the same story. Even they thought it was a bit crazy, and they are only 4 and 5 years old. Hey, I had a school conference with her once and she told me my daughter was SO bright. I don't have a daughter! I like the old goat, but I think she has lost it a bit when it comes to handling this age group. But, thank God, she has a great teacher's aide so I really don't worry about it."

Janet juggled the conversation in her mind as she sat at The Call later that morning. She phoned Kitty, who was fresh from the tennis court on her day off.

"Think we could do a little journalistic work on teachers' tenure, Kitty?"

"Sure, go down to the Administration Building and talk to Maria Watkins, the community relations coordinator. She works part-time in that job; she used to be an English teacher at the high school but left when her kids were small. I know her from tennis. She'll help you out. She's great."

It couldn't be the same Maria Watkins, Janet thought as she sat facing the short, well-groomed School Board spokeswoman. The woman would have nothing to do with Janet's inquiries about school personnel.

"Why do you want to know about the backgrounds of our teachers? We have a good school system."

Janet repeated herself: "I want to write a story about tenure and I need background information so I can interview the newer teachers as well as the veterans."

"Why is The Call becoming so sensational?" asked Maria Watkins.

Janet was livid as she wrote---and verbally repeated---"sensational" in her notes.

"Let me get this straight," Janet said in a strong voice. "The schools' community relations person will not provide requested information from a community newspaper that she calls sensational. Do I have it straight?"

"Personnel matters are not subject to access laws," shouted Watkins.

"I am cognizant of the law, Mrs. Watkins. I know that personnel meetings can be conducted outside a public session. But the public---those of us who pay taxes to pay teachers and PR people in the school system---have every right to know the ages, educational background and salaries of municipal employees. Do you ever read our column, The Finish Line, in The Dunfield Call?"

"Yes, all the time, " answered the schools' spokesperson, beginning to look upset.

"Make sure you read it Friday morning. This conversation will be the topic of that column. Once again---did you say sensational?"

Janet walked out of the Administration Building and ran the four blocks to the paper. She phoned Kitty at home again.

"Did you say that Maria Watkins was great---or an ingrate?"

Then she fired off a column that was the sensational story of the week in Dunfield.

CHAPTER 13

KITTY AND JANET FACED EACH other across the lunchroom-size table that formed one side of their private "office" in the rear of The Call building. They resembled a pair of Rodin's "The Thinker" statues as they leaned their arms on the table to support their pensive faces.

This was the official weekly "business" meeting for the two editors/publishers, and both hated it, particularly when the topic turned toward money. Neither could balance a checkbook, and the prospect of balancing the books for The Call was beyond their desires, so Hank and a part-time bookkeeper handled most of the chores.

Janet produced the latest typed figures of their financial situation---"we're not quite in the black yet. We have to increase our ad base."

"What do you mean, our ad base?" asked a smiling Kitty. "Is that one of your sports terms from the old days?"

"You, Kitty Moran McIntyre, our St. Agnes salutatorian, you don't know what ad base means? Let's get down to BASE tactics and straighten you out. What do you think ad base means?"

"Well, "said Kitty, "it's probably a watering hole you go to after a Red Sox game. Like an extra base."

"No."

"OK. It's Revlon product you put over moisturizer. You know, ad base."

"Nope."

"Janet, I quit. What's the darn ad base we have to increase?'

"We have to sell more ads---that's all."

"What's that got to do with a base? You are getting real fancy with your publishing terms. Pour me another glass."

The weekly meetings, held late on Wednesday afternoon after the paper had been completed and sent to the printer, always featured a bottle of good Chardonnay and cheese purchased at The Vin Etc., a nearby wine store that advertised in The Call. Sometimes a glass or two of wine played havoc with the serious intent of the session, as Kitty and Janet digressed off topic in their conversation.

"Sell more ads?" commented Kitty. "We better keep the ones we have. How many advertisers have we lost because of the Rec Commission and teachers' tenure stories?"

"Only one, really. The drugstore. The men's store that pulled its ad—that place closed last week anyway. But the good news is that Ken got Klines Department Store in Hartford to take out a full page every week. Klines never advertises in weeklies."

"How did Ken do that?' asked Kitty.

"They called us," said Janet. "Apparently the president of Klines---I think his name is Rafter---moved to Dunfield lately and he's a bit disgusted by the school taxes. He read our column about Maria Watkins refusing to give us information, and he told his ad manager to call us. That guy told Ken that Mr. Rafter---or whatever his name is-- says to keep up the good work."

"Wow, that calls for a toast, Janet."

Kitty raised her long-stemmed glass and said: "To The Call. Bound for Success. Take The Finish Line and Ad Base!"

They started laughing in tandem.

"I'll beat that," said Janet. "To The Call. Off the wall. But what a ball!"

Arm in arm, they exited their den of journalism iniquity and headed to the hectic scenes at their respective homes.

The arrival of scores of press releases from local groups proved problemsome for Kitty and Janet, who refused to print articles that did not represent proper journalism. When the paper had been owned by the Rockwells, people would write up information about varied events and the copy would be printed intact.

"We need to abide by a specific style," Kitty said as she changed a poorly written release from the Women's Club of Dunfield. "When it says twenty women, we change it to the number 20 as most newspaper styles do, and we ax subjective adjectives. I doubt if the Women's Club crafts party was "marvelous,' as this press release says."

"Should we even put in follow-up stories about these kind of events?' asked Janet. "We already had an article about the crafts party coming up, and we need not stretch it out for another piece. We could just use a photo from the event with some cutlines underneath the picture."

They were particularly upset by the so-called leads on most press releases as the writers had no idea how to start an article for publication.

Kitty started reading from a release from the local Boosters Club about its scholarship dinner the week before. The article started with a sentence that said "The Boosters Club held its annual scholarship dinner last week."

"No kidding," said Kitty. "We had an article last week that the event was coming up. You never write a lead that could have been written before the event. You start with something that happened at the event. Some news. As in who the devil won the scholarships??"

Then the release alluded to the committee and the number of people in attendance. Five paragraphs down were the names of the local students who were awarded scholarships.

"Good God," said Kitty, as she rewrote the lead: "*Seven Dunfield residents were honored Sunday night when they were named recipients of this year's scholarships donated by the Boosters Club.*"

She then listed the names of the award winners and cut out the long list of committee members who had been mentioned the previous week.

Janet seconded the complaints being verbalized by Kitty and then suggested that they invite publicity and PR chairmen from local groups to an evening workshop to learn how to write proper releases and take photos for their organizations.

"Good idea," said Kitty. "I can put together a handbook with examples and other information."

The response to an ad announcing the free PR workshop proved surprising to The Call owners.

"Fifty people...can you imagine that? They want to come to the two-hour session to learn how to write a press release?" commented Janet.

"Wow---at least we know that 50 people read our house ads," answered Kitty. "And we better make sure this is a good event."

They booked a community room at St. Matthew's Episcopal Church.

"It better be at no cost for all the free publicity we have done for my church over the years," said Janet, who nevertheless offered to pay a minimum price to rent the facilities. "Guilt feelings. I need all the prayers I can get and don't want to step on any clerical toes."

Hank and Tim volunteered to assist their wives by handling registration at the door.

"Hey, we have a financial stake in the paper so let's help out," Tim said to Hank a few days previously when the pair met for a few brews at The Dunfield Pub.

Hank agreed "as long as we can head here for a beer as soon as the workshop is over."

The two men were enjoying their stints at the PR workshop as they welcomed many people whom they knew from around the town. Even Maria Watkins, the hard-to-get-info-from public relations director for the local schools, was in attendance.

"Guess she wants to make sure her releases are written the way our wives like them," said Tim, who numbered Maria among his dental patients.

Kitty began the session by showing an example of the beginning of a poor press release:

On Tuesday, October 10, the Area Senior Women's Bowling Club will have an event at 12 p.m. at Will's Bowling Center on Central St. Doctor Hilda Grayson will speak about ways to prevent injuries from bowling the wrong way.

"Take a look at the mistakes in those sentences," said Kitty to the workshop attendees. "Never start with a date. Don't say there will be AN event---what is the event? And we don't use 12 p.m. or 12 a.m. in stories---noon or midnight are correct. The word Street should not be abbreviated unless the exact street number of the building is listed. Doctor is Dr. and how about saying she is an orthopedic surgeon?"

Kitty then showed a screen shot of a visual with the lead of the piece as it should be written:

Dr. Lucille Grayson, a Hartford orthopedic surgeon, will discuss "Injuries from Bowling" at a meeting of the Area Senior Women's Bowling Club on Tuesday at noon at Will's Bowling Center, 12 Central St., Dunfield.

With Clara's help, Kitty and Janet had used presentation software to create slides that showed how to write credible press releases and how to take photos that would be considered good choices for publication.

Kitty showed group shots that she said "really are not the best but are acceptable as we want to feature people in our area and they do love to be photographed. But please make sure that in the cutlines under the picture you do not identify the people in the group as standing left to right."

A woman in the audience raised her hand.

"So we should name them from right to left? I really have never seen it done that way in a paper."

"Oh, we want you to identify them starting From the left," answered Kitty. "But do not write 'from left to right.' There is only one way to go from left---to the right--- so all you need to write is 'from left.'"

Almost the entire assemblage nodded their heads as if to say they never even thought of that.

"We are making headway, aren't we?" Janet said after she explained how to submit stories and photos to the paper.

As attendees asked questions, they also complimented Kitty and Janet for their teaching skills.

"I am really learning a lot," said a woman representing a local garden club.

The others in attendance applauded as Kitty and Janet smiled. Even their spouses, sitting in the back, seemed impressed.

The tone of the workshop was positive and amiable---until The Call Girls focused on letters to the editor. Janet explained that The Dunfield Call receives lots of letters but that most do not get published.

"We allow a certain amount of space for letters and we select those that are most relevant to issues that have been covered in previous issues of the paper."

A heavyset, stringy-haired woman stood up and pointed to the instructors.

"I don't like your paper."

Kitty and Janet looked at the devilish grin on the woman's face and said nothing as the latter continued: "You should publish the articles I send in."

"Excuse me---and who are you?" asked Janet.

"Mildred Hofcaw. Females Forever's public relations person."

Kitty interjected: "Oh, you are the one who sends us those lengthy op-ed pieces that call for women to take over the world."

"Yes, and you do not print them."

"Let me explain what an op-ed piece is," said Kitty. "It is..."

"I know what it is," said the argumentative woman whose organization's activities had outraged many in the area. "Op-ed means opinion editorial and it is written by people who send them in."

Janet was staring, obviously steaming that this woman would dare take over the instruction.

"You are wrong about that," she said. "Op-ed means opposite the editorial page. That was its original meaning when these pieces were placed on the second page of the editorial section.

And we do print op-ed pieces that we accept or solicit from individuals who espouse particular opinions and are credible writers. Example: our schools superintendent wrote an op-ed piece last week in which he called for parents to pay fees for their children to participate in sports activities. The article was well-written and timely. It abided by our rules for length and required no changes in style or grammar. The piece carried the byline of the writer and noted at the bottom that he is the Dunfield Schools superintendent."

"Yeah, you agree with the schools guy so you print that," said Mildred Hofcaw. "You don't agree with Females Forever's philosophy so you don't bother to print my writings."

Janet was getting more incensed by the second. In the back of the room, Hank turned to Tim and said: "I can see fire in my spouse's eyes."

"As a matter of fact, I don't really agree with the schools superintendent," stated Janet. "In fact, we are considering writing an editorial to express our reservations about the proposed sports fee. And by the way, an editorial is the opinion of the paper rather than of an individual. It carries no byline."

Mildred Hofcaw kept at it.

"I just think you fail to print my writings because you think that we in Females Forever are crazy or something."

Janet and Kitty watched as the workshop audience in concert yelled: "YES."

With that, Mildred Hofcaw stormed out of the meeting room as she continued her rants against the paper.

"Wow, I did not expect that," Janet said to the assemblage as she continued to explain the specifics of an editorial page.

As she and Kitty ended the session, though, they were given a standing ovation by the others.

The following afternoon, Kitty and Janet sat down in their office to mull the events of the previous night.

"I am exhausted after that workshop," said Kitty. "But I think we were a hit."

"Well, when Hank Watson spends the rest of the night just praising us, you know we did just fine," answered Janet. "And he was happy that we did not tell Mildred whats-her-name to go stuff it," she said.

They were smiling when Clara's voice came through the intercom.

"Some women here to see you," she said. "From last night."

"Send them in, as long as it is not that Mildred person," answered Kitty.

A few minutes later, two women, who appeared to be in their early 50s, walked in carrying flowers and a few bottles of wine.

"We are friends through the Women's League that runs the thrift shop on Elm Drive," said a woman who introduced herself as Jane Morris. "I was at the workshop last night because I handle the shop's publicity. This is Carrie Clarkson who was there for the Dunfield Bridge Club. We want to thank you for the great workshop. And you handled that feminist woman with such tact. She seems to show up everywhere from the School Board to the library meeting to carry on about her mission."

Kitty and Janet invited the visitors to join the publishers for "some of that good wine you brought and maybe give us some suggestions as we move forward in this newspaper business."

Carrie asked about whether The Call sought any columnists.

"Why? You interested?" asked Janet.

"I started a blog on bridge," she said. "I hope someday it can be a column."

"Well, we are in no position to pay columnists..." Janet began.

"I am not looking to be paid," said Carrie. "Bridge columns are well-read and I want people to read what I write," she smiled.

Janet looked at Kitty and said: "Fine with me. We can run it in paper and then, when we do get into the online edition, probably move it there."

"Fantastic," said Carrie as the group toasted her.

Jane said she was putting in a lot of hours at the Women's League Shop after cutting back her work hours as a nurse.

"At St. Mark's?" asked Kitty.

Jane sighed as she explained that "Now I only work one shift a week to keep my skills up. That place has changed, and not for the better, under new ownership."

CHAPTER 14

—

ALMOST A YEAR INTO THEIR newspaper ownership, Janet and Kitty were the talk of the town. With the help of freelancers, they were covering Town Council as well as the School Board meetings, and sessions of the town's commissions. Their stories about the nepotism displayed by the Recreation Commission resulted in the resignation of three members of that board, and the School Board was reassessing its tenure regulations after The Call's two-part series about Dunfield's teachers.

"We seem to be forcing some changes in Dunfield," said Janet as she and Hank dined one evening with Kitty and Tim at Dunfield Country Club.

The freelance staff included women who had left their fulltime professional posts to raise their children and were enthused about writing for the paper. Harriet Lyman, who was in her early 50s, was a former Manhattan assistant prosecutor who married a Dunfield widower with two teenage sons and exited her New York job to move to Connecticut. Right away, she became active with the high school PTO and was writing the organization's press releases when Janet emailed her and said: "You are such a good writer. Ever consider doing some reporting?"

Turned out that Harriet had been editor of her college newspaper in Virginia and thought that writing for The Dunfield Call would give her a chance to meet more people.

As they devoured the Saturday night fare at the club, Janet and Kitty told their spouses that Harriet was becoming an integral part of the newspaper ranks.

"We pay her next to nothing and she does not seem to care," said Janet. "She really enjoys covering meetings and her legal training is paying off. She should win a state journalism award for the housing stories."

Harriet was upset after covering her first Housing Authority meeting. Two of the board members had their eyes closed for most of the session and she noted that in the piece she wrote.

At the next meeting of the Authority, the members discussed the way that the town would handle some housing issues. Harriet thought the approach was in conflict with state law, and spent the next day in checking out Connecticut regulations relative to fair housing. Her curiosity proved right, and she penned a two-part series about the town's illegal approach to housing laws. The county prosecutor called for an investigation and the Housing Authority chairman resigned immediately.

As he sipped another glass of Pinot Grigio at the club, Hank remarked to Janet and Kitty that he enjoyed reading the new food column in The Call. It was written by a nutritionist whom Janet met in a weekend yoga class.

"You know what," said Janet. "I think she should write a column about fish."

"Why?" asked Kitty as the men listened.

"Look what you are eating. Tilapia! Did your mother ever cook that? Did anyone's mother ever cook that? Is this fish for real? Or is this one big fish story? I do not think tilapia have ever been near an ocean. I think they grow on tilapia farms in China or somewhere like that."

As they chuckled about the arrival of tilapia into the American culinary scene, the Watsons and McIntyres were approached by a tipsy Frank McDow, the town councilman and construction magnate who had fired Tim's dad a decade before.

"So you are causing some sensation in our colonial town, huh?" asked the bespectacled McDow.

Kitty and Janet said nothing.

"Well, you certainly caused problems for the Housing Authority and that makes me damn angry," continued McDow.

"Was Harriet Lyman's reporting inaccurate?" asked Kitty, who had edited the pieces with a fine-tooth comb.

"Who cares?' said McDow as those at surrounding tables looked up from their expensive meals to follow the heated dialogue. "We need a town paper that supports the town. You people just want to cause trouble. What the hell is wrong with you two ladies?"

An irritated Tim stood up and told McDow to "walk away from this table. Now. You obviously have had too much to drink, as usual. You are not going to berate my wife or Hank's wife."

McDow raised his fist as if to start a fight when a veteran waiter stepped in front of him, took McDow by the arm and walked him out of the room. From the table next to the McIntyres and Watsons sat a group of octogenarian widows and widowers who frequently dined together. One was a former state senator who commented quite loudly: "I love reading The Dunfield Call since those two young ladies took over. And that Frank McDow is one nasty guy. No wonder his wife kicked him out last year. Funny part about it is that his old man, Jim, was a good friend of mine and a really good person. People liked to work for Jim and then this guy Frank, his only son, took over about 10 years ago when Jim died unexpectedly and right away Frank started firing people and hiring cheap labor. A disgrace."

Upon hearing the remarks, Tim looked at Kitty and said: "We know all about that. I will always be incensed about what the jerk did to my dad."

CHAPTER 15

—

JANET AND KITTY CELEBRATED THE one-year anniversary of their ownership of The Dunfield Call by inviting about 25 female friends to
dinner at Farmers' Bistro, a new restaurant on Main Street. The
eatery had been opened by twins Gretchen Morris Wakefield and
Heather Morris Rush, Dunfield natives who had graduated from
a New York culinary program before working in various restaurants in Manhattan and Boston. While visiting their parents over
Christmas, they discovered that a space was available on Main
Street for a restaurant, so they moved back, with spouses and
young children, and were living in rented townhouses not far from
their new venture. Their husbands, both of whom had online sales
jobs, worked part-time with them when they could.

The bistro had opened in May with a special feature added
to the business--- in line with a growing national trend, Farmer's
Bistro instituted a weekly Health in a Box business; customers
would sign up to receive each week a box of "surprise" vegetables
and fruits from local farms. Janet signed up immediately and
would bring her box to the Call offices for anyone who wanted to
pick from the contents.

"It isn't as if I am going to eat that kale," said Janet one day. "Be
my guest."

"You don't read your own paper," laughed Kitty. "Our nutrition columnist devoted five paragraphs last week to the healthy benefits of kale."

"I'm turning green just thinking about it," said Janet in her comedic voice. "And the Swiss chard can go back to Zurich for all I care."

At the anniversary festivities at The Farmers' Bistro, Janet told the attendees that "it is good thing this is a BYOB place as we could not afford to buy drinks for this gang." She and Kitty had raided the wine racks from their respective homes and everyone was toasting the pair on the journalistic success of their initial year as publishers. Harriet Lyman told the assemblage that she never thought she would be swapping a prosecutor's career for part-time reportorial work, and said "I love working with Janet and Kitty and Clara and the others. And I still have time to take a crack at writing a novel."

"Our own Linda Fairstein?" asked Janet, alluding to the former Manhattan prosecutor who pens best sellers.

Harriet had just won first place in the state Newspaper Association's contest for weekly newspapers for her Housing Authority stories and admitted to those at the dinner that, while she first was a bit apprehensive about marrying and moving to Connecticut, she now "loved" Dunfield, its residents, and her life.

Alice and Annie, two friends from Kitty's tennis league, had recently told her that they were a gay couple and wanted to know if their impending nuptials would make it into the newspaper.

"Sure," said Kitty told them. "We would be happy to do that. We changed all those old, stupid rules."

Now, at the dinner, the pair mentioned that they had set a wedding date and that they were happy that their photo would make the town paper.

"Well, there is a charge for wedding announcements, you know," said Janet.

"How much?" asked another guest.

"Eighty dollars," said Clara, who handled the social pages.

Before the gay couple could say anything, five-dollar bills were flying out of the purses of the guests, who apparently were making a statement that they wanted to see the wedding photo make the paper and thus would cover the costs.

Alice looked at Annie and shook her head.

"Guess we have to invite this whole group to our reception."

"Yep" came the response in concert from the wine-chugging women.

The hostesses capped off the gourmet meal with a black forest cake, a tribute, as they told attendees, to the fact that The Call finally was in the black financially. The diners cheered as Janet and Kitty made that announcement.

"You are our BFFs," said Janet, "so we wanted to share the news with you. But the men are still part of this celebration. We are using our husbands' charge cards to pay for this soiree!"

The publishers also announced that they would begin to concentrate on designing a digital edition of the paper and on strengthening their presence on social media. A few of the women even volunteered to help with the launch.

"But," said Kitty, "we will never stop providing the best coverage of Dunfield and other towns, no matter what the cost to us personally."

She never thought they would ever face that reality.

CHAPTER 16

———

WHEN IT CAME TIME FOR Timmy McIntyre to start first grade, Kitty and Tim opted to send their only child to St. Philomena's, the school associated with their Catholic parish. Ironically, the Vatican had removed Philomena from the list of saints but most U.S. churches named after her had kept the name.

Kitty had spent her grade school years at St. Phils, as the alumni called it, and was glad that it had not met the fate of so many other Catholic schools that had closed as operating costs escalated and the number of nuns in America decreased dramatically. Sister Camilla, the principal and one of but three nuns on the faculty, was enthusiastic to have Mary Moran's grandson as a pupil; as a young nun, Sister Camilla had worked closely with Mrs. Moran who headed the grade school's PTO when Kitty and her two younger brothers were students at St. Phils.

Sister Camilla had risen to the administrative ranks after years of teaching seventh grade.

"I give that woman credit for teaching me the fine points of grammar," said Kitty to Janet one day as she returned from a meeting with Sister Camilla. "I think of her a lot when I am editing copy."

Kitty still worked a six-hour evening shift twice a week on the copydesk at The Hartford Tribune and Janet still penned her "Oh, Mother" column that the Tribune was syndicating to about a dozen American papers. They considered their Trib work to be in the vein of continuing education as they got to keep up with what they called "the real world of journalism." Their hope was to turn The Dunfield Call into a small island of good journalism but they were cognizant that weekly newspapers needed to be mired in service journalism to keep alive. In effect, they had to provide information about everything from the results of soccer games for 10-year-olds to the activities of local clubs. Any immersion into hard reportorial work was difficult with a staff of a few but they were making headway with the help of part-timers like Harriet.

Janet appeared to be weighing her partner's remark about grammar.

"You just gave me an idea, Kitty. I think we should write our "Finish Line" column next week about the plummeting of grammar skills in this country."

"Well, we can salute the Catholic schools for trying hard to retain the teaching of good grammar, even with sentence diagramming," said Kitty, "especially at St. Phils. I learned so much there about the importance of grammar and I am tempted to write a handbook that shows all the lousy grammatical and usage errors I find in articles. I just read a sports article in the New York Times that said the amount of players was increasing in the NFL. I think they meant the NUMBER of players unless they weighed them all."

"Wow. That is why you are a copy editor extraordinaire, Kitty. You should be teaching all this stuff."

"As a matter of fact," answered Kitty. "You hit the nail on the head."

"And that would be a cliché?" laughed Janet.

Actually, Sister Camilla had made an appeal at a St. Philomena's PTO meeting for parents to volunteer for a myriad of possible duties to help out the school. As the cost of paying lay faculty members increased, the school needed to use volunteers in lieu of paid workers to help in the library, the lunchroom, and even with some instruction. Kitty already had made sure that the school's funding campaign had generated a lot of coverage in The Dunfield Call and wondered what she could do to help at the school. After all, her time was limited with her work at The Tribune and The Call. But Sister Camila came to her after the PTO meeting and said the teachers in the upper grades---sixth through eighth---wanted to put out a newsletter or newspaper with the students once a month. But, as Sister explained, most of the teachers had been trained in teaching process-based or whole language writing; they had little experience with formal journalistic writing. So Sister Margaret wondered if Kitty might be able to give the teachers a workshop to acquaint them with some of the basics of reportorial writing.

Kitty told Janet about the request.

"So what did you say?" asked Janet.

Kitty answered "of course" and took off on a verbal dissection of writing instruction in general.

"Remember I have a master's in English and when I was in grad school I wanted to scream every time a professor went into ecstasy over process writing stuff. I got sick of hearing about Chomsky and others. I swear that even the professors had no idea what they were talking about. They want kids to start writing in kindergarten, and not worry about mistakes. They say the students will learn about grammar and spelling and usage as they get older. Baloney. Compare it to baseball. Timmy can play in that T-ball league where the kids don't know the rules. They just hit the ball and run. But wait until those kids get to Little League. They will be taught the rules and the nuances of the game. It is not happening in writing instruction and that is why the Tribune gets applications from people who think they can write but cannot. Remember the old way of teaching writing? I got that in Catholic school. First we learned the parts of speech and then we wrote sentences and then we put those into paragraphs. Only then could we write an essay. It took years. In seventh grade we diagrammed sentences until our fingers hurt."

Janet shook her head.

"Remember, I went to public school through eighth grade. My mother, who was trained as a teacher, was not happy with the instruction, so that is why she made me go to St. Agnes Academy for high school even though we are not Catholic. And believe me, I was behind from the start. But those nuns kept focusing on good grammar and good writing, and I had to learn. And I wound up in journalism school! Of course I am lucky I even graduated from St. Agnes after that canoe race article."

Kitty announced that she was putting together a two-day program for the teachers. "And I am naming it NEWScamp. Network for Effective Writing Skills camp. Tim suggested it. What do you think, Janet?"

"Wow. Trademark it. This could be another one of our side entrepreneurial ventures."

CHAPTER 17

———

WELL INTO THE SECOND YEAR of the Janet/Kitty publishing stint, the paper was gaining recognition throughout the state as a top-notch weekly, especially after it had editorialized successfully against the re-election of Frank McDow and another incumbent to the Dunfield Town Council. Despite having the endorsement of a number of groups, the men were handily defeated by two young women who had campaigned door-to-door in a grass roots undertaking. In an editorial backing the female candidates, The Call noted that "it's time to start crushing the arena of nepotism on town committees. Let's start with the Council members who run the town."

When the women won, they wrote a letter to the editor in which they pledged to make all council activities transparent as possible. They also lauded The Call for its "extraordinary" contributions to the town.

The debut of The Dunfield Call's online newspaper proved a boon to the financial status of the publication. For months, Clara Woodruff scrapped her editor's duties for an hour or two a day to check out successful online editions of weeklies across the country. She also set up Janet and Kitty with a video conferencing interview from a top media research group official who provided advice as to the best approach to initiate an online presence. In some cases, newspapers only offered headlines and links to their top stories. Others had the entire issue as published put into online form in what was termed a digital edition. Janet and Kitty opted for the latter route, and, on the advice of the media guru, hired a small Hartford-based firm to get the entire paper "up" online and to assist with promoting it as well as their print edition through varied social media outlets.

"This social media stuff is driving me nuts," said Janet one day after attending a PTA meeting at the public school that Marta attended. "The principal told the parents that we should check Facebook every day to see what was going on at the school. So, after Ken, our great ad salesman, showed me how to do it, I opened a Facebook page and all these people want to be my friends. Good god--- some of them put stuff up---or post stuff, as it is called---detailing every little thing they do every day. And I'm like a fool looking at these posts because I cannot believe people want their lives unveiled like that."

"Ken told me that we need to get a Facebook page and a Twitter account for The Call for promotional purposes," Kitty stated as she shook her long blond hair. "Heck, I'm still trying to figure out how to use voicemail on my cell phone."

The birth of the digital Dunfield Call came after 10 days of steady promotion through the paper's Facebook pages and its @dunfield-call Twitter pages. Ken designed a full-page ad that was put in the paper the week before the launch. He called it a "house ad;" that basically meant it was placed by the owners and would not generate a penny for what normally would be a $1,000 charge.

As they imbibed Chardonnay at the owners' weekly "business" meetings in the back office, Kitty complained to Janet that the paper needed revenue, not free house ads.

"Quit whining," responded her partner.

"You are telling me to quit drinking this wine?" asked Kitty.

"Not really, but no whining while wine-ing!"

"Was that rule in our business plan?" Kitty laughingly inquired.

"Sure," said Janet in her comedic persona. "We probably picked it up from the Bible. Remember the wedding at Cana and the parting of the seas? You know: The Days of Whine and Moses."

"Cripes," said Kitty. "You have got to do standup, Janet."

From the outset, the digital edition attracted thousands of "hits" that meant that many of those living in Dunfield and the nearby towns were reading the paper online. Nevertheless, the print editions were still selling well; in fact, the circulation was at all-time high. Kitty and Janet attributed that to the fact that the world of all-digital newspapers had not proved as successful as first expected in the media world. AOL's venture, The Patch, had not caught on in many areas, and some so-called hyperlocals were experiencing trouble. It seemed that people still wanted to read weekly newspapers and cut out photos and articles about their family members.

"The Finish Line" appeared to be the biggest hit of all. No matter where Janet and Kitty went, people would comment about the most recent offerings in the weekly column. Their writing about grammatical problems and poor writing skills generated a score of letters to the editors, mostly from older readers who were appalled at the way their children and grandchildren struggled with penning perfect sentences.

One letter, from a teacher who did not appreciate the column, had them laughing out loud. The writer was an English teacher at Dunfield Middle School; she was defending the way she taught students how to write. She said she was ANXIOUS to attend an upcoming statewide conference about holistic writing and suggested that the authors of "The Finish Line" also register "to learn about good writing skills."

"I think she is EAGER, not ANXIOUS to attend," laughed Janet. "And what the hell is holistic writing?"

"Don't ask," said Kitty. "That was another crazy thing they taught in my grad classes."

"I am surprised they passed you at UConn," said Janet.

"Those profs gave me a lot of trouble, especially when I asked to do my thesis on writing coaches at American newspapers. They said it was a poor topic. I said: 'What do you want me to write about? Flatulence in the writings of Shakespeare?' They actually said that someone already did that. Finally they agreed to my topic and it was clear that I better do a good job or else."

"And you did, Kitty," stated Janet. "I was there at the Editors' Society conference in Manhattan when you received a special award for your work on newspaper coaches."

"But I still did not get an A grade for it. Those English profs were too proud to admit they had a distaste for anything related to journalism."

As they waxed poetic about the plummeting state of writing, they were interrupted by the sound of Harriet Lyman who had entered the office in a state of agitation.

"What is the problem?" asked Kitty as Harriet sat down at one of the desks provided for staffers.

"Who is St. Mark?"

"The guy who wrote some Gospels?" responded Kitty.

"Have no idea," said Harriet, "but he would no doubt be embarrassed to have a lousy hospital named after him."

The lawyer-turned-reporter then proceeded to explain what happened to her next-door neighbor, Will Kloster, a Hartford insurance company executive in his early 50s. Two days previously, his wife took him to the emergency room at St. Mark's Hospital because he was feverish and coughing a lot. The doctors said Will had pneumonia.

"Mind you, he was in the emergency room for almost six hours before anyone bothered to treat him," said Harriet. "That's an aside."

Janet shook her head: "Hey, I know all about that from my sprained ankle when I was pregnant and from the twins' birth when the Trib science writer was so upset by the place that he wrote an article about emergency rooms. And I cannot forget when I got the neck brace the night before we closed on the purchase of the paper and the place was crazy. By the way, I know Will Kloster; he plays golf with Hank at the club and I have had dinner with him and his wife, Edna."

"Well, he did play golf," said Harriet. "No more. He died this morning."

She proceeded to explain---and complain.

Will's wife, Edna, asked for a private room for Will and, after she signed papers that the Klosters could afford the rate differential from a semi-private room covered by insurance, her spouse was put in a room on the fourth floor. About two hours later, at 8 p.m., a doctor came in to see Will.

"Not Will's primary physician," said Harriet. "A doctor called a hospitalist. Apparently that's a specialty, believe it or not. These doctors work in the hospital and take care of patients who are admitted by other doctors."

"I call them chart doctors," said Kitty, "as I dealt with them when my father was hospitalized last year in Boston. All they did was read some charts. They did not know my father at all."

Harriet said the doctor at St. Mark's reportedly asked Will a few questions and mentioned that he would talk to Will's doctor and discuss what medicines should be ordered. During the next hour or so, only once did a nurse come into the private room. The nurse took Will's temperature and gave him some pills ordered by the hospitalist. Edna stayed until about 9 p.m. and returned the next morning about 8 to see her spouse. Will told Edna that he got little sleep and only remembered once seeing a nurse come in and check on him. It looked to Edna as if Will was getting weaker.

"Edna said that her family always insisted on private-duty nurses for any family member in the hospital, and she decided that she would request them," said Harriet. "She went to the nurses' station and spoke to the supervising nurse who apparently almost chuckled and said 'you really don't need private nurses. We can handle everything.' Edna said she would feel more comfortable with private duty nurses but the head nurse continued to discourage her."

Edna and her oldest son spent the day with Will and, when he needed something one of them would go to the nurses' station and then a nurse would show up. They stayed until about 10 at night and, since Will was asleep, they left.

"Edna was worried about Will and returned to the hospital at 7 a.m.," continued Harriet. "She walked into his room and tried to wake him. And he was dead."

No one at the hospital would tell Edna when a nurse last checked on her spouse. Edna got the impression that a wall of silence was implemented quickly after she ran, screaming, down to the nurses' station.

"My god, did he die from the pneumonia?" asked Kitty. "And what time did he die?"

"Well, Edna had the sense to demand an autopsy and has no results yet," said Harriet. "This whole thing is unbelievable and I think someone should start looking at that hospital."

She was visibly upset and kept mumbling: "This is not right."

Janet looked at Harriet, turned to Kitty and practically yelled: "Is it time for The Call Girls to move into investigative journalism?"

CHAPTER 18

———

WHILE KITTY ENJOYED HANDLING COPY-EDITING duties two nights a week at The Hartford Tribune, she decided that it proved to be getting a drag on other things in her life, including work at The Call. So, two-plus years into the purchase of the weekly paper, she gave up the Tribune part-time gig; Janet continued to write her "Oh, Mother" column that was syndicated through the Tribune. They still collaborated on their "FinishLine" column in The Call and that continued to generate a lot of feedback in the Dunfield area.

Now that she had more hours to spare, Kitty headed full-force into setting up her NEWScamp for the St. Philomena middle-school teachers. Sister Camilla was so enthusiastic about the venture that she asked Kitty to allow a few middle-school teachers from other local Catholic schools to attend the two-day workshop.

"Fine by me," Kitty told the nun. "Just hope they learn something."

"And include me on the roster," said Sister. "I love the idea of learning from you."

Kitty scheduled the NEWScamp for two successive Saturdays in a computer lab at St. Philomena's School and kicked off with her approach to putting together a journalistic piece. Much of her instruction would be based on what she learned from writing coaches whom she interviewed for her master's thesis.

"Remember these letters," she said. "C-O-D-E."

She explained that the letters stood for Collect, Order, Develop and Edit. Step-by-step she explained how a reporter has to **collect** information from a myriad of sources, determine in what **order** the story should be written, **develop** the story as it is typed into shape, and then **edit** the piece to ensure it is accurate and follows an expected newspaper style.

"Editing---maybe I am biased," said the veteran copy editor, "but I think it is the most crucial step in the process. You must ensure that an article is error-free and follows the particular style of your publication. And by the way, writing an article is not a linear process from start to finish; sometimes you are into the editing part and discover some more information is needed so you have to go back to the C---Collect information."

Kitty watched as the 15 teacher-attendees took notes furiously; she had told them they to take hand-written notes because notetaking "is a skill---and what reporter would bring a computer to a fire he is covering?"

"Take lots, not jots," she said about notes, as "it is easier to cut information than to add things if you fail to take enough notes."

Practicing interviewing skills proved to be a highlight of the initial day's activities. First Kitty showed a video of a press conference with a governor and pointed out how some reporters asked good questions and others asked questions that were poor from a journalistic perspective.

"One thing you learn in journalism classes is to avoid Yes or No questions as they elicit little information," said Kitty as she pointed on the video to a broadcast journalist who asked the governor "Do you like working with the new state attorney general?" The governor had answered: "Yes" and said nothing else.

Kitty said "the reporter should have asked: 'How would you assess your working relationship with the new attorney general?' and then the governor would have had to expand on an answer."

She then took on the role of actress Meryl Streep at a press conference and answered questions from the teachers acting as reporters. Kitty was impressed by the serious questions posed by the group.

The teachers then headed to the computers and wrote articles stemming from the make-believe press conference as Kitty walked around and discussed how the stories should be written.

At the end of the first day, she gave an assignment: the teachers either could attend a meeting, like a School Board or Town Council session, and write it up as if it were for a weekly paper, or they could interview "someone interesting" and write a feature about that individual.

"Send the stories to me by email as soon as you can, and I will have them ready for you for our session next Saturday. And, you know what, we might even publish some of them in The Call."

Throughout the following week she kept in contact with her teacher-pupils who were eager to send emails with questions about their stories. One teacher had covered the monthly meeting of the Dunfield Historical Society, the oversight body for the town museum housed in an old farmhouse. It turned out that a few Society members, led by a professor in his 40s, wanted to revamp the old barn on the property so it could accommodate classes in everything from candlemaking to colonial cooking. But the oldtimers in the organization would have nothing to do with the idea that any structural change be made on the farmhouse or the barn.

Kitty opened the email from the teacher who covered the meeting and read:

After a raucous three-hour meeting of the Dunfield Historical Society on Tuesday night, the organization's longtime president declared "I resign" and stormed out of the session at the Sythe Farmhouse.

Kitty was amazed. Not only was the writing good but the story deserved front-page treatment. She turned to Clara and said: "Run this article with the headline: **Historical Hysterics: Society Prexy Quits**."

She then called Janet at home and reported that "this NEWScamp project is not only fun but I think it can be a boon for us. I am getting some good stories."

Kitty opened the next emailed story from another teacher in NEWScamp. She had interviewed a nurse practitioner. Kitty read the story and picked up the phone again. This time she called Harriet Lyman.

"I want you to read something. Check your email."

Harriet drove to The Call offices after reading the story that Kitty forwarded to her. She was shaking her head as she remarked: "We have to do something."

The feature centered on the nurse practitioner's disillusionment with her former job---at St. Mark's Hospital. While not condemning the facility itself, she had inferred that problems at the hospital had led to her resignation and her move to a job in pharmaceutical sales.

"Will Kloster's death brings a lot of things into perspective," said Kitty. "We really need to do something."

The Call's move into the investigative ranks was beginning to jell.

CHAPTER 19

———◆———

EVEN THE HOT SUMMER WEATHER failed to deter Kitty and Janet from their forays into local journalism. But it also resulted in their taking up a new sport: golf.

"I am sick of listening to Tim come home from a golf game and tell me about every shot he had," said Kitty to Janet as they finished putting out the paper one day.

"Ditto for me and Hank," said Janet. "He was grilling steak and kept saying he had to stop slicing all the time. I thought he was taking about the meat."

Figuring it was easier to play golf than listen about it, the pair decided to sign up for clinics at the country club. Considering that they both were athletic, they figured it would be an easy sport to learn.

Several weeks later, they devoted their "Finish Line" column to their debuts into the world of golf. In part, they wrote:

Just call us hookers. Of course, we've been called a lot worse since we purchased The Call. Now we are immersed in trying to learn the game of golf. And together we hit some of the best hook shots in Connecticut.

We thought the game was easy---just hit a little white ball straight ahead and then putt it into the hole. After a series of lessons (God have mercy on assistant pros Phyllis and Kevin at Dunfield Country Club), we started playing some nine-hole rounds.

We are now experts. Not at golf, but at tree identification. On the second hole we together hit a total of seven trees---including a gigantic oak, an ugly sycamore, a pretty birch, a maple, and a few others. Those trees could be the root cause of our lousy golf. Literally.

We are better at using an iron (at home) than using an iron on the fairway. And that is saying a lot since both of us have put holes in our spouses' shirts.

The witty writing, now a landmark of the Janet-Kitty literary partnership, generated a lot of response---almost 50 comments on the paper's website. One reader said he killed a bird in flight while driving a ball and that his wife, with whom he was playing, insisted on burying the bird before they continued playing:

"Every time we play that hole now, my wife stops and prays over the darn bird. That bird gets more prayers than our parents who are buried across the road in Dunfield Cemetery."

Harriet Lyman, who had played golf for a few years before moving to Connecticut, joined them a few times on the course, but her presence usually was to encourage the two editors/publishers to expend more time in looking into St. Mark's Hospital. Her neighbor, Edna Kloster, was determined to file a lawsuit against the hospital after an autopsy showed that her spouse, Will, had not been given a number of pills prescribed by his physicians.

Harriet also had spent a number of hours in speaking with the nurse practitioner interviewed by one of the NEWScamp teachers.

"I am a frustrated former prosecutor," said Harriet to Kitty and Janet as they downed Chardonnay at the clubhouse after one of their golf rounds. "And you are both seasoned journalists. Can we delve into this hospital situation?"

Janet and Kitty said that, while they wanted to immerse the paper into an investigative mode, they were ill at ease in focusing on the town's lone hospital. Their mothers had been members of the hospital's auxiliary and they knew older town residents who had served on the hospital board before the facility was sold to a firm that owned several hospitals in the Northeast.

"It sounds as if it is something that we should be doing," said Janet, "but should stories of this type not be the bailiwick of the dailies or a television station? You know, outfits with big staffs and other resources. If we pursued this, Harriet, you could use information from your neighbor and from the nurse practitioner, correct?"

"Yep," said Harriet.

"And who else?" asked Janet.

"Well," said Harriet. "We would have to interview officers of Lerod Health Enterprises, usually called LHE, the outfit in Boston that owns the hospital. And the new board president at St. Mark's His name is Frank McDow."

Kitty cringed.

"He is the new head of the board of trustees at St. Mark's? The one that canned my father-in-law? The guy who got voted off Town Council with our help? Holy Christ. That does it---we are going big time into investigating what is going on at St. Mark's!"

The threesome then vowed to sit down a few days later and sketch out their approach to the reporting.

"I think we can get a few of those teachers from NEWScamp to join us on a part-time basis," said Kitty. "I knew that darn class would be valuable. And Clara will be glad to get into the research end of this. She is becoming a master of Internet information."

Thus began a months-long, in-depth look into the practices at St. Mark's Hospital. The Dunfield Call was transforming itself from a typical weekly that provided information to the locality to a publication that elevated its journalistic endeavors.

CHAPTER 20

———

THE END OF SUMMER TRANSLATED to a two-week vacation at Cape Cod for Tim and Kitty. They rented a home on Ridgedale Beach near Chatham for what was touted as the cousins' get-together. Two of Tim's first cousins and their families rented cottages nearby, and they all spent a few hours together each day at the beach. It was there that Kitty grilled Tim's cousin, Frank, a Manhattan-based neurologist, about Lerod Health Enterprises. Turned out he had an ex-colleague who went to work a few years previously for a Western Massachusetts hospital that later was bought out by LHE.

"He lasted a year," said Frank. "He said that LHE started cutting back on purchases of equipment and supplies. Then some of the nursing staff was axed. One day he refused to perform an operation because he said there was not enough medical staff in the room but there was some guy who was dressed like a doctor but was a salesman for some ridiculous surgical device that LHE was being hounded to buy. My friend threw out that guy and then walked the hell out of the operating room and quit. The anesthesiologist never started his work---he walked out, too. They both work in Boston now."

Kitty called Harriet in Dunfield and said she had the names of two ex-LHE employees who might speak to her for the series of articles that the paper was preparing. Janet and Kitty had trained Harriet to follow all traditional reportorial work in securing information. While it appeared that LHE might be a less-than-ethical firm, the realm of objectivity still had to be paramount from the reporters' perspective.

The Cape Cod vacation for Tim and Kitty also featured a weekend visit from Janet and Hank and their four offspring. Timmy McIntyre was overjoyed to introduce Marta, Molly, Brett and Billy to his shovel-and-pail activities on the beach.

"I am digging to China," he told them.

"Is China at the bottom of the beach?" inquired 5-year-old Marta.

"On the other side of the world," answered Timmy.

"How long should we dig?" she asked.

"About an hour, I think," he said.

Janet and Kitty laughed as they watched their children discuss the geographical wonders of the world.

"I used to dig to China when I was a kid on this beach," said Kitty. "Must be a family thing."

"Nope," remarked Janet. "My mother had us digging to China, too."

They debated the reasons as to why reasonable adults would try to convince innocent children that they could dig to China.

"Why not Bhutan or Tanzania?" asked Janet. "Or maybe Nepal or Tibet."

"We need to write a 'Finish Line' column on this," Kiitty responded.

So, the next issue of their column in The Dunfield Call opened with:

So you thought the Big Dig was the years-long effort to improve tunnel traffic in Boston.

Wrong.

Try the beaches of America where unsuspecting children utilize large plastic shovels to dig in the sand.

Seriously, how many of us, in our childhood days, endured hours of digging to a Communist country courtesy of encouragement from our mothers?

"Why don't you dig all the way to China?" was the frequent refrain from our moms when we were kids on the beaches at The Cape.

Never mind that the closest our moms came to China or its culture was the takeout menu at Hunan Delite in Dunfield.

The column called for readers to recall their China-digging exploits and the response was overwhelming for a weekly newspaper. Thirty-five readers contributed email stories about their digging to China. One man said that, when he was about 5, he was digging to China in his backyard and hit some broken pieces of porcelain. He showed them to his mother who said: "Yes, you have hit china. REAL china!"

The best response came from Hunan Delite in the form of an order of General Tso's chicken and brown rice delivered to The Call with a note: "Thanks for the free publicity." Ken Masterson saw the message and headed to the Chinese restaurant to convince the owner to advertise.

CHAPTER 21

———

HARRIET AND CLARA WERE MOVING head-on into their hospital-related research. Their Internet searches had yielded a lot of data about lawsuits against U.S. hospitals. Janet and Kitty had made it clear that the paper's objective was to publish a series of articles that would focus mainly on St.Mark's but would include background and related materials about hospitals and hospital chains in general. The project would be a staff-based undertaking, with Clara heading research efforts, Harriet and Janet handling most of the writing, and Kitty editing all of the copy.

The key component was to secure credible information about St. Mark's. Harriet's neighbor, Edna Kloster, was more than willing to discuss her spouse's death at St. Mark's. Edna had hired a well-known Hartford lawyer to represent her in a lawsuit she planned to file against St. Mark's. That lawsuit would be the genesis for the first article in the series as it would basically announce that a town resident had filed a negligence suit against the lone hospital in Dunfield. The subsequent articles would deal with the information that The Call had discovered about the problems at St. Mark's and its parent company, Lerod Health Enterprises.

The staffers knew that the nurse practitioner who had been interviewed for a feature piece by a NEWScamp participant would be a superb source, but Harriet would have to convince her to go on record for the articles. They also needed to secure solid quotes and stories from unhappy former patients at St. Mark's. And they had to try to get some St. Mark's executives to speak to them, but knew that would be a difficult scenario.

One focus would be the management of Lerod Healthcare Enterprises and its purchase of St. Mark's. That had been the impetus for a lot of changes---not good ones---at the local hospital.

In a sense, Kitty and Janet felt a bit sad that a hospital that had been such a special part of the town no longer was a symbol of pride. But their experiences---and the seemingly unnecessary passing of Will Kloster---made them realize that their move to serious journalism was now central to their entrepreneurial mission.

"I made an appointment to see the PR person at LHE," Harriet told her two bosses after the summer vacation ended. "So I am heading to Boston."

Janet laughed.

"Now we are sending our staff out of state? Do we have enough funds for that, Kitty?"

"How would I know?" Kitty answered. "Your spouse handles the books. Ask him."

Harriet said she did not care. If need be, she would finance the trip herself.

"I saved when I was single and then sold my condo in Manhattan," she smiled.

"Enough said," commented Janet. "One sold condo in the New York City market is worth a lifetime in Dunfield. But we are a real business, I think, so we will pay for your one-day trip up the road to Boston. Good luck."

Harriet's brief soujourn in Beantown proved futile. LHE's vice president of PR was uncooperative from the moment Harriet entered her office.

"When I called and asked to see her, I said it was about an article for our paper about St. Mark's and I think perhaps she was counting on a feature story. By the time I got there she had figured out that it might not be a flattering piece so she would offer no information about the company. She handed me a media kit that had been distributed three years ago when LHE bought St. Mark's. Press releases and background material. I had already seen all of that when I checked the old issues of The Call and saw the press releases---printed word-for-word, by the way, by the former owners of this paper. Since LHE is a public company it puts out an annual report that probably no one reads because the language in annual reports is a turn-off. The PR flak gave me a copy of the report and it says the company is making money. A lot of the officers and top shareholders are doctors, by the way."

Harriet explained that LHE is buying small hospitals that no longer can survive alone because of the rising costs of technology and insurance.

Clara had looked into the specifics of the purchase of St. Mark's and discovered that, along with the hospital building, LHE picked up other Dunfield properties. One was an Art Deco structure that had housed St. Mark's Nursing School that had closed in the early 1980s. It was now headquarters for a social services agency. Also included in the purchase was an old Victorian home that had served as the residence for a group of nuns who had been on St. Mark's staff several decades ago. For the past 20 years, this structure was used as a nursing home.

"According to my sources, both buildings are going to be razed so LHE can build apartments or condos that will be available not only for staffers but the general public. Remember, LHE is a profit-making firm."

"Cripes," said Kitty. "That nursing home is great. My grandmother lived there for a few years before she died."

Janet was puzzled.

"Wait a minute. If these sales are planned, has the current St. Mark's board not released information about that yet?"

"Why would they do that?" answered Harriet. "It would be one big controversial mess."

"Well," said Janet. "Our articles will generate controversy, for sure."

CHAPTER 22

————

WHILE THE HOSPITAL STORY WAS their main consideration at the time, Kitty and Janet still found interesting possibilities in other stories.

A press release from the local Y had them in stitches. It said that a veteran tennis instructor was going to have a one-hour class to teach youngsters ages 1 to 8 about the game.

"Seriously," said Janet. "A one-year-old in a tennis class. We need to cover that one."

Less than a minute later, Kitty saw an email come in from one of the teachers who had been enrolled in the NEWScamp program.

"She has a year-old son and wants to sign him up and then write a story about it. Great. Her name is Kathy Barrett and she is finishing her master's in English and is considering a journalism career. We will have a volunteer reporter there."

When Kathy filed the story several days later, Janet said it was perfect for the main page of the features section of the paper.

"Who would not get a good laugh over this one?" she said to Clara who was laying out the paper.

In part, the story read as follows:

My 15-month old son, Trent, followed a tennis ball around the courts while saying "Hi, Ball. Hi, Ball."

And I kept thinking that is exactly what I would like to be drinking at this point.

After seeing an article about a tennis class for kids 1 to 8, I signed Trent up for $10 because I could not believe that a child that age could learn anything about a sport.

I thought the whole thing might be a racket.

Actually, Trent picked one up and promptly smashed it to the ground. Thank God it was not the head of another youngster.

The rest of the story detailed Kathy's humorous interviews with other parents and her proclamation that the instructor was a model of patience. The accompanying photos, of kids hanging over the net, added comic relief to the piece. Kitty penned the headline: **Tennis: All About LOVE for Youngsters!**

"Why is it that love means zero in tennis anyway?" she asked out loud in the office. "I would LOVE to know."

Clara said "it has something to do with the shape of an egg."

Kitty stared at her: "I never should have asked."

When the article was published, it was picked up by a national tennis magazine that reprinted it. Kathy Barrett was, as Janet said, "loving every bit of her journalistic work."

Into its third year, The Dunfield Call was expanding its staff. In addition to editor Clara, ad salesman Ken and bookkeeper Iris, the payroll included part-time reporters Harriet Lyman and Candy Smith, an ex-journalist-turned homemaker. A growing number of freelancers, including Kathy Barrett and a few other teachers from the NEWScamp ranks, were paid per story. Sales manager Ken

Masterson kiddingly would remind Kitty and Janet that he was the lone male at The Call and they would remind Ken that the paper's two paid interns were male UConn students getting credit for their work.

"We need more space," Janet said to Kitty at one of their weekly wine-fueled business meetings.

"Is that good or bad?" answered her partner. "More people. More salaries."

Janet said that Hank, who continued to handle the money end of the business, was praising Ken's work as the ads were increasing big-time. The women figured the paper was dong well as the editions were beginning to require extra pages to handle the ads, and the online version also was attracting ads.

Yet the pair seldom focused on the monetary side of their newspaper venture. They were keyed into running a good news operation and covering Dunfield politics, its varied town commissions and local organizations. They loved writing "The Finish Line" each week and Janet still enjoyed penning her syndicated "Oh, Mother" column.

They agreed---as they toasted themselves with Chardonnay at the weekly meeting---that the office was not large enough to accommodate the staff.

"One of our leases is almost up," said Janet, alluding to the three apartments they rented on the second floor of The Call building that they owned. "Let's convert it to OUR offices."

A month later, a local contractor who regularly advertised in the paper, revamped an apartment into spacious offices for Janet and Kitty.

"Wow, this looks great," said Tim as he stopped in to pick up Kitty on their way to Timmy's soccer game.

"We feel like executives," said Kitty. "But I still love the nuts and bolts of this newspaper work."

Within the next hour, she had a chance to do some unexpected reportorial work. As she and Tim sat in the bleachers at Timmy's soccer game, they watched in disbelief as one man, upset that his 7-year-old son did not get enough playing time, lobbed profanity-laden verbal insults at the volunteer college-age coach. Then the argumentative father took a swing at the young coach. Tim joined other parents who walked onto the field to confront the nasty father. A lot of yelling ensued.

Kitty simply took out her cell phone and videotaped the fracas.

She put the photo on the front page with a story about the incident, and added the link to her video on the paper's website.

The parents were delighted but not the nasty father. He stormed into The Call office with a letter to the editor that took Kitty to task---in horrendous language. Kitty filed it away in her "Holy Cow" letter drawer. When the letter was not printed, the combative man called.

"Why the hell did you not print my letter?" asked the man.

"That awful letter?" answered Kitty.

"Listen," said the guy. "You might not like my letter but you have an obligation to print it. It's the law."

Kitty laughed to herself. She wanted to say he was a dumb idiot but she acted professionally.

"There is no law that says we have to publish a letter to the editor. We own this paper. Buy yourself a paper and publish whatever you want. Anyone can start a paper. You need no license."

He hung up. He then posted his letter and some anti-Call remarks on a town Facebook page. Many people added comments---all in favor of The Call. One person wrote: "I was at that soccer game and I have never seen a parent act like that. Do us a favor, buddy, and move out of Dunfield."

Two weeks later, he did.

"Oh, the power of the press and the Internet," chuckled Kitty upon hearing the news.

CHAPTER 23

———

HARRIET CONTINUED FULL-FORCE INTO THE St. Mark's stories-to-be. Through the nurse practitioner who had left the hospital staff, Harriet got the names of several other disgruntled ex-employees. A few refused to be interviewed, saying they were not interested in airing their dissatisfaction. But one pair---a married couple---provided an inside look at how St. Mark's was operating under the flag of Lerod Health Enterprises.

Bob and Shirley had met in nursing school where the former was the lone male in the class. After Bob spent two years as an Army nurse with stints in Iraq and Afghanistan, the couple married and both took posts with Lerod. Assigned to St. Mark's, they worked mostly in the emergency room. Shirley said she could "write a book" about the place.

"One night there was a multi-auto accident on 95 and some of the passengers were brought to St. Mark's. But we were understaffed; a few nurses had called in sick and I knew they were going to a Red Sox game. Anyway, we could not handle the influx of patients. The emergency room supervisor, a big woman with a big voice, did not have the brains to insist that other nurses be reassigned from some of the hospital floors. That is what most hospitals do---send out a Blue Code and staffers take on different assignments. Heck, some nurses are sitting at desks and filling out paperwork on some floors. But no---we got no assistance. We had to handle the load ourselves. Some of the injured waited on gurneys for a few hours before being looked at. Awful. Just awful."

Bob was so upset by the situation that the next day, he went to the office of the medical director and complained.

"He sort of shrugged his shoulders and said the hospital would do better the next time. I was furious," said Bob. "I told them that the hospital is a sham. Then I quit---before they could can me. Shirley quit, too."

Bob returned to school to become a physician's assistant and Shirley took a job at a UConn clinic.

"We did not lose faith in our profession," said Bob. "We lost faith in our employers."

Harriet underlined those words in her notebook, realizing that they would make a great pullout quote when the stories were published.

When Harriet relayed what she learned from Bob and Shirley, Janet's ears perked at the reference to the oversized nursing supervisor.

"She must be the same one who was there when I sprained my ankle while I was pregnant with the twins. That place was a nightmare."

"How did you sprain your ankle?" inquired Harriet.

"A turkey fell on it."

"What?"

Janet said: "It's a long story."

Janet counseled Harriet to go over her notes to make sure everything was accurate and that nothing could be construed as potentially libelous. The fact that Harriet was a lawyer made things easier on everyone.

"And let's get our thinking caps on about the art we need to accompany the stories," said Janet.

Harriet was puzzled.

"We need artwork?"

Janet smiled. She forgot that Harriet was not familiar with all of the terms associated with newspaper work.

"No---photos or graphs or anything outside of copy per se can be construed as art in this business. We will need photos of some of those people you interviewed and of LHE hospitals and perhaps some graphs with data. Just keep all of that in mind. Harriet, we will talk later---after Kitty and I get back from Bermuda."

"Did you say Bermuda?"

CHAPTER 24

—◆—

JANET AND KITTY DECIDED THEY needed a vacation---alone---without spouses or offspring or colleagues.

"Let's go somewhere to play golf," said Janet. "Nanny Annie can stay with my kids."

Kitty agreed. The shared nanny would stay at the Watsons to help Hank out with the children. and Timmy McIntyre would go to the Watsons after school until his dad could pick him up.

The Call Girls, as they continued to term themselves, decided that a quick trip to Bermuda would be their choice of taking a break while having time to discuss the future of their newspaper ventures.

After a short flight from Bradley International, they sat in the President's Club lounge at Newark Liberty, awaiting their plane to Bermuda.

"I swear I know that guy over there," said Kitty as she looked at a couple seated nearby.

She kept shaking her head as she mentally ran through names of people she knew.

"Bingo," she uttered to Janet. "He went to dental school with Tim. They came to our wedding. God, I cannot remember their names but I know they were from Scranton."

"Scranton, as in Pennsylvania?" said Janet. "I dated a guy from Scranton when I was at Mizzou."

"You're kidding," remarked Kitty. "Who goes to the University of Missouri from Scranton?"

After getting up her nerve, Kitty walked over to the couple and said: "I'm Kitty McIntyre. I think I know you."

The guy stood up.

"Tim's wife, right? Wow---great to see you. We were at your wedding."

"That's it," said Kitty, "and I am trying to remember your name. Kevin?"

"Yes. Kevin McCarthy. This is my wife Megan. We live in Bergen County here in Jersey."

"No more Scranton?"

"We still love our hometown of Scranton," laughed Kevin, "but Megan took a nursing job in Jersey and I joined a dental practice here."

"Actually, I recently quit my job," said Megan. "Could not stand working at the hospital I was at."

Kitty began to think. Harriet had mentioned that LHE was buying up hospitals in the New York metropolitan area.

"Who owns the hospital you worked at?" asked Kitty.

"Lerod Health Enterprises bought it last year. Major disaster."

Kitty explained that she and her traveling companion, Janet, owned a Connecticut weekly newspaper that was gathering information about LHE because it had purchased the lone hospital in the town and lots of problems were surfacing there.

"Can we have a reporter interview you?" asked Kitty.

"I would be happy to give my views on LHE or, as we fondly called it, Lousy Hospital Environment. But you will have to wait until Kevin and I return from China."

"Wow. You are waiting for the flight to Shanghai? We've never been there. Well, we did try to dig there, though," chuckled Kitty as she wrote down Megan's contact information to give to Harriet for the interview.

After 18 holes on Bermuda links, Kitty and Janet were convinced that they were improving as golfers.

"Hey, we both parred that fourth hole," exclaimed Kitty.

"Yep, we are pretty good at 90-yard shots," laughed Janet. "I never saw such a short par 3."

As they sat later in chairs at the hotel pool, they declared that they were loving this break from The Dunfield Call and from their active young offspring. The main topic of discussion, though, centered on their choice of a restaurant for dinner.

"Italian food or lobster?" asked Janet.

"I just want Bermuda fish chowder," her business partner answered. "Had a lot of it last time we were here."

That was nearly two decades previously when the pair came to Bermuda's Semester Break Week. Kitty was still reeling from her mother's death and she convinced Janet to come all the way from the University of Missouri and meet with four other classmates from their St. Agnes days. The week was somewhat of a blur as they downed many beers, but they never forgot being thrown out of a beachside pub one night for dancing on the tables.

The group could not get cabs back to the place they were staying so the girls slept in the front yard of one of the colorful Bermuda cottages. Then the police arrived and threatened to arrest them unless they left the island that day. And they did---two days ahead of schedule after switching their tickets for first-class seats.

"Remember, we used your credit card and charged the tickets to your mother," said Kitty.

"She had a fit," said Janet. "Good thing I was out in Missouri when the bill came. I stayed out there that summer and worked on The Missourian because I was afraid to face her. But now we are back in Bermuda as serious entrepreneurs."

"Serious? Hardly. Janet, I am up for another Chardonnay," said Kitty as she walked to the pool bar.

After a nap, they headed to a restaurant for fish chowder and lobster--and a serious discussion about the path their business would take.

Kitty thought The Call should be the basis for other undertakings. She was convinced that NEWScamp could be extended with workshops for teachers in the Hartford area and with summer programs for middle and high school students.

"We can train teachers who took the NEWScamp workshops already to help us establish the summer NEWScamps for students all over the state," she said. "I can put together handbooks that we can sell as part of the deal."

Janet had been thinking about her "Oh, Mother" column that was being distributed through a California syndicate that was making more money for it than she got paid by The Tribune for writing it.

"Why don't we start our own syndicate?" asked Janet. "I am pretty sure I can convince a few journalists to syndicate through us. Plus, our nutrition columnist would be a good choice, and we have our bridge columnist who would be happy to be syndicated. We need to hire someone to help set this all up, though."

They wrote down their ideas in the NOTES apps on their cell phones and vowed to engage in more extensive discussion about them when they returned to Connecticut.

"In the meantime," said Kitty, "we need to break 100 on the golf course, Jan."

"For how many holes?"

The trip also proved fodder for their next offering of "The Finish Line" as they offered their opinion about the state of being airline passengers in the 21st century:

Squished.
How often do you utter that word?
Probably every time you fly coach.
We are not in the ranks of even the slightly overweight and we could hardly fit in our assigned seats on a recent vacation.
Now imagine a 300-pound woman settling into an economy seat.
Well, we aren't imagining; she was sitting between us.
One of us booked the window seat and the other chose the aisle seat. We hoped that the middle seat might remain empty.
Almost---until the standby passengers were allowed on the flight from Newark to Hamilton, Bermuda. This weight-loss program flunkie was assigned to the middle seat in our row.
Believe us, "squished" does not do justice to our situation.
Forget the armrests. They disappeared under her arms, or some part of her physique.
For fear we might chuckle, we did not dare look at each other. Actually, we couldn't. She blocked our views.
Halfway to Bermuda, the woman said: "It's a bit crowded, isn't it?"
No kidding, lady.

The column continued with the authors asking what happened to the two-seat rule that reportedly was being imposed on airlines: if you are too fat for one seat, you buy tickets for two seats. They also thanked God they were not flying to Europe or Asia.

Janet and Kitty expected a bit of flak for their description of their seatmate.

"I think we may hear from obese people who sympathize with this woman or who think the two-seat rule is not good," said Janet.

But what they received were many complimentary comments on their web page and in letters to the paper, except for a letter to the editor from the public relations head of the airline. He wrote that "there is no two-seat rule on our company's planes. We do not want to discriminate. We hope that heavyweight people under-stand that they need to consider purchasing two adjacent seats, but we will not mandate that."

The Call published his communiqué and then added a com-ment penned by Janet: "Your airline is discriminating---against us passengers who buy tickets for full seats and then are forced to have someone else take up part of our space."

She got no response from the airline but lots more online com-ments on the subject.

It was clear to Kitty and Janet that "The Finish Line" had be-come the most popular feature in their paper.

CHAPTER 25

———

FOR MONTHS, HARRIET CONTINUED TO secure as much information as possible regarding St. Mark's and Lerod. Janet and Kitty also conducted interviews. Kitty discovered that Rick Carter, owner of the historic house that was the scene of the famed "Siege of Dunfield," had quit the St. Mark's board of trustees after Lerod took ownership of the hospital. He was more than happy to describe an executive board meeting when chairman Frank McDow said he would be bidding on the construction contract for a new addition to the hospital.

"It was an unbelievable conflict of interest just to suggest that," said Carter. "I was on the board for 15 years and enjoyed helping St. Mark's. But that did it. I quit that night after giving it verbally to McDow. At least he withdrew his bid before I left the room. Unfortunately we were in executive session so your reporter was not there."

Harriet interviewed Megan McCarthy after the latter returned from China, and learned that Lerod increased charges substantially after buying the New Jersey hospital where she worked. Janet also spoke at length with Jane Morris, one of the two women who had brought flowers and wine to The Call the day after the publicity workshop. Janet remembered that Jane said she was a nurse who was unhappy at St. Mark's but worked once a week to keep her hand in the profession. Jane proved to be a fountain of information as she described sloppy paperwork being handed in by staffers and the continuing decline in staff morale. She copied a day's report from a nursing floor and showed it to Janet who immediately found some discrepancies in the material.

Harriet found a Rutgers University study that noted that large for-profit hospital firms were charging a lot more for services than non-profit facilities. She decided to look into St. Mark's charges for emergency room cases. Knowing that she would not get cooperation from hospital officials, she checked public records of the town's Rescue Squad to find out names of people who had been transported to St. Mark's emergency room and contacted several of them. A few said they paid no attention to the hospital bills as they were covered by insurance, but one woman provided her St. Mark's bill for being treated after she slipped on ice and sprained her ankle. That same day, several other Dunfielders fell on black ice and were transported by the Rescue Squad to nonprofit hospitals in Hartford. Harriet compared the bills and it turned out that St. Mark's charged 30 percent more than the nonprofits did.

Courtesy of Harriet and Clara and others, the information-gathering had yielded a lot of material, so Janet and Kitty decided to start putting the stories together. They decided they would publish the stories right after Emma Kloster filed suit against St. Mark's over the death of her spouse, Will. The Klosters' lawyers had waited nearly a year to file the lawsuit as they wanted to amass a lot of data about St. Mark's and LHE. That information, to be released as part of the filing, would be additional ammunition for the stories to be published in The Call.

As she edited each story, Kitty carefully studied the words with an eye to ensuring that the piece was accurate and followed the standard Associated Press style used for all The Call stories.

Initially, Kitty and Janet figured the investigative report would constitute a four-part series. That meant, though, that since The Call was a weekly, readers would have to wait a week for each article over a month's time. So the publishers decided that the stories would be printed in a special section to be inserted into one issue of the paper. Although Clara and freelancers had helped with research and writing, the two publishers decided that only they and Harriet would get bylines. In the event of any legal repercussions, they would take the heat. The week prior to publication, they promoted the special section about St. Mark's in the regular issue and in the online paper. Almost immediately, Frank McDow and the heads of Lerod started emailing the publishers and warning them that any problem with the stories would result in a lawsuit.

Harriet kicked off the main story in a way often associated with Wall Street Journal feature articles: focus on one person at the outset:

> *Dunfield resident Will Kloster could not shake a cold last winter, so he was admitted to St. Mark's Hospital after going to the emergency room there.*
>
> *The diagnosis?*
>
> *Pneumonia.*
>
> *Concerned that Will seemed to be getting weaker, his wife, Emma, asked that he be assigned round-the-clock nurses for his private room at the family's expense. The hospital rebuffed the request.*

When Emma went to visit him at 7 a.m. the next day, she found her spouse dead in bed. Hospital employees used what Emma called "a wall of silence" when she and other family members insisted on knowing when staffers had checked on her spouse and what medications he had been given.

Two days ago, the Kloster family filed suit in Hartford against St. Mark's and its owner, Lerod Health Enterprises, (LHE) for "negligence in the death of Will Kloster."

St. Mark's, for decades a non-profit facility that was a beloved part of the Dunfield community, has undergone major changes since it was sold to LHE. That Boston-based firm continues to buy hospitals in the Northeast, and to escalate patients' costs while employing many disgruntled staffers.

The rest of Harriet's main article focused on what happened to Will who went from being a healthy golfer to meeting his demise in a matter of days. Harriet described the lawsuit in detail and outlined some of the problems that patients and employees had faced since the hospital ownership changed.

"Powerful," said Kitty as she perused the story as it was set for publication.

Other articles included interviews with former Lerod doctors and nurses, as well as with unhappy ex-patients. Janet wrote an article on the backgrounds of those serving as trustees at St. Marks's; two of them lacked high school diplomas. Some material was presented on graphs that Clara had put together to compare costs at area hospitals. Photos of St. Mark's, its emergency room entrances, and the other buildings it owned were included with the material. The newspaper could not get permission to take photos inside St. Mark's but a former employee furnished her own photo at a nurses' station where she had worked, and several people, including

Megan McCarthy, the New Jersey nurse, and two former St. Mark's board members provided their photos for publication along with interesting quotes about their experiences.

Kitty penned an editorial that lashed out at Lerod for not getting involved in community-sponsored activities. The piece also called for the town to insist on better medical care with fair charges.

The special insert also included "The Finish Line" in which Kitty and Janet explained why the paper had undertaken the investigation into St. Mark's:

Our parents were born at St. Mark's.
We were born there.
Our children were born there.
Their children will not be born there.
St. Mark's closed its maternity section two months ago in what was called a "cost-cutting" move.
Well, we are not moved by the changes in our town hospital. We are miffed that the medical care, in the opinion of many Dunfield residents, has deteriorated. Just ask Emma Kloster whose spouse died in circumstances that have resulted in a lawsuit for negligence.
The current owner, Lerod Health Enterprises, is planning to close the nursing home long tied to St. Mark's. That facility has been a great comfort for many who needed end-of-life care and that includes some members of our families.
Today's special section, researched in depth by The Call, focuses on the changes at St. Mark's and the operation at that hospital and others in the LHE portfolio.
We welcome your responses at www.dunfieldcall.com

As for the emails they had been receiving prior to publication from Lerod executives: Kitty and Janet decided to publish them to show

how threats were being made against them. Clara, with help from a UConn graphic arts intern, did a first-class job of laying out the special section that ran without ads. But the main part of the paper included more ads than normal as Ken Masterson convinced advertisers that the investigation section would result in increased sales of The Call.

Not only was circulation up but the response to the special section was extraordinary.

Janet and Kitty got calls from many Dunfielders who saluted the paper for its first foray into investigative journalism. On the day of publication, the two publishers hosted a late afternoon reception at The Farmers' Bistro to celebrate the work done by Harriet and the staff. Harriet was the recipient of many kudos emanating from the group of friends who came to toast The Call staffers. When Emma Kloster walked in, she announced proudly: "You girls are the best. Well done!"

Janet and Kitty were surprised---and delighted---when the Hartford Tribune editor, Michael Collins, called and asked if he might reprint the main article from The Call.

"Wow---that's a plus," said Kitty. "Our work is getting recognized."

"We didn't get that much recognition when we worked at the Trib," laughed Janet.

What really shocked the duo was the lack of a response from St. Mark's or LHE afer the stories were published.

"I expected at least a nasty email or phone call blasting us," said Janet as she and Kitty sat with Harriet in the office several days after the stories were printed. "I figured McDow would start screaming after the threats he made in the emails before the stories came out."

"Well, I heard he blasted us when he was at the bar at the country club on Saturday," Kitty responded. "Some of Tim's golf buddies heard him take off on us. He called us the Dunfield Disgraces. Said something about our paper heading to oblivion."

"I doubt if he used that word," answered Janet. "He would not even know what it means."

The response came a week later in the form of a lawsuit, filed by LHE and St. Mark's, against The Dunfield Call for libel.

"Bullshit libel," said Kitty. "I edited every word and made sure our sources were legit."

Still, the paper was about to enter into expensive litigation that could bankrupt the operation.

Normally funny Janet almost cried when she read the lawsuit.

Harriet tried to reassure her.

"The stories are solid. We made sure of that. And truth is a defense for libel. Everything we wrote is truthful and attributed."

"But how are we going to fund a lawsuit, even if we win?"

Kitty reminded Janet that they had taken out a libel insurance policy with a press association.

"Up to $100,000 coverage as I recall," said Janet. "LHE probably has a legal team that will drag this out just to clear our bank accounts. The sad part is that we are in the right. And now we have to pay to use that right. I feel as if I got hit with a right hook."

"You need a good lawyer," said Harriet. "Not yours truly as I am part of the group being sued."

Kitty said they should call Jack Mason, who handled the legal side of the purchase of the paper, and see what he thought.

Mason told Kitty and Janet that they really needed a libel specialist to handle the case, and gave them a few recommendations. In the end they chose Mary Quinn, a New York-based lawyer who also held a Connecticut license. Harriet knew her and agreed she was a perfect choice but did note that Mary's law firm was an expensive entity. Quinn met with LHE lawyers with the hope they might drop the lawsuit because, she stressed to them, they would not win the case. It was clear to her, as she reported to Janet and Kitty, that LHE did not care; the firm was out to use the case to bankrupt the small Connecticut weekly.

CHAPTER 26

———

ONE DAY, A FEW MONTHS later, Janet and Kitty sat in their office at The Call while sharing their lunch choice---pizza with extra cheese.

"We better get used to this type of fare," said Janet. "This might be all we can afford after paying the legal fees and court costs. And maybe selling the paper and this building to do that."

The case had been simmering for weeks and everyone agreed that LHE had no chance of winning a defamation suit against the Call. As Harriet said, the firm's deep pockets were being used to send a message to others in the media---don't mess with us or we will bankrupt you.

"The Dunfield Call is being used to make that point," she said.

Janet and Kitty were sick of depositions and discussions with lawyers, as well as explanations to anyone who brought up the subject of the lawsuit.

The paper itself was doing well; advertising was up and the circulation went up 30 percent after The Call added a few near-by towns to its coverage. Subscriptions to the online edition also had increased. Interestingly, some of the new online readers were college journalism students who had been assigned to read The Dunfield Call. Kitty and Janet attributed this to the national coverage that the lawsuit was garnering in publications aimed at journalists and journalism students.

The expansion of NEWScamp had become a moneymaker for the entrepreneurial Call publishers. Kathy Barrett, who had written the humorous tennis-for-babies story and had covered a number of meetings of local municipal agencies, took over the NEWScamp part of the business after finishing her master's and scrapping fulltime high school teaching to begin doctoral studies at UConn. Several schools contracted with The Call for teachers' workshops.

And a NEWScamp program for middle and high school students had proved so popular that it was offered after school in five towns. Kathy recruited English and journalism teachers to teach the courses, and Janet and Kitty stopped by frequently to assist with instruction. An article in a national journalism magazine about NEWScamp resulted in inquiries from throughout the country and Kathy was determining how the program could be expanded to far-off places.

To focus on syndicating Janet's "Oh, Mother" column, Janet and Kitty aligned with the Hartford Tribune to syndicate a number of columns to papers across the country. A Tribune employee handled most of the work while Janet and Kitty solicited columnists to join the new entity.

"Smartest way to do it," Kitty said to Janet as they finished their pizza at their weekly business meeting. "We have enough work to do here at The Call and we can always re-negotiate our agreement with the Trib."

Just then Janet's cell phone rang and she picked it up to find Nanny Annie at the other end.

"Brett fell and landed on the edge of the piano. His head is bleeding but he is alert. I called 911."

"We'll be there," said Janet, and she and Kitty drove quickly to the Watson home just as a police car was leaving with 4-year-old Brett in the arms of an officer.

"They are taking him to St. Mark's," yelled Ann as the publishers pulled up to the house.

Kitty looked at Janet.

"St. Mark's? Dear God."

"We have to deal with it," said Janet as they headed to the hospital and into the emergency room.

Brett was in an examining room and was crying for his mother when Janet ran into that area. He was alert and a doctor was holding a towel over the forehead of the 4-year-old.

"I think a few stitches will do it," said the doctor, who also was making sure to rule out a concussion.

Brett stopped crying and told his mother that "I hit the piano. But I am okay."

As the doctor continued to treat Brett, Janet walked out to the waiting area where she found Kitty reading behind the cover of a magazine about urology.

"Incontinence?" asked Janet, trying not to laugh.

"I am hiding as I don't want anyone to see me here," said Kitty.

Janet said she had to fill out insurance papers and Kitty kiddingly asked if Brett might be treated under an assumed name. Janet walked over to a staffer who began to take information. A few minutes later, Janet returned to Kitty and said:" I left my wallet at the office. I told that lady I have full coverage under Hank's insurance from the bank, and she keeps telling me I have to prove it."

"Ridiculous," said a miffed Kitty. "People rush to emergency rooms without thinking about insurance. The hospital should know that. I have a blank check in my wallet. I will pay the bill and you can deal with the insurance company later."

Janet turned to return to Brett when her eyes focused on the nursing supervisor.

"Oh, God, Kitty," she said as she pointed to the oversized woman who was the same one in that post when Janet was treated for her turkey-on-ankle injury. "She's the one that the husband and wife nursing team---I forget their names---blasted in our St. Mark's report. We did not put in her name, though."

"But we quoted their description of her as a big nurse with a booming voice," said Kitty. "And I doubt if anyone else could fit that description. I am going to keep my head in this magazine. I am learning about something called interstitial cystitis."

A brave Brett never flinched as he got stitched while his mother promised to buy him chocolate ice cream on the way home, forgetting she had no money on her.

Kitty paid the bill---all $1,000 of it for four stitches in the ER. When the receptionist saw the name McIntyre on the check, she asked Kitty if she was related to the dentist.

"My spouse."

"My dentist," said the woman. "He convinced me to get a subscription to your paper and that is where I read the stories about St. Mark's."

Kitty simply nodded. Then she turned around and practically pushed Janet and Brett out the door.

"Pray that this does not make it up the chain at LHE," said Janet.

"But we have some ammunition," laughed Kitty.

"Really? What?"

Kitty said she went into the ladies' restroom near the ER and found that it was "filthy. With a trash can overflowing. I took pictures with my cell phone camera."

"You go girl," said Janet. "And thanks for paying the hospital bill. Now I need to borrow some cash to buy chocolate ice cream."

Janet and Kitty always abided by the rule "to get to them before they get to you." They had used it when the wrong picture of a bride was printed one time. As soon as they saw it and before the post office delivered the print editions to subscribers, they called the bride's family and apologized and said the correct photo would be published in the next edition, and the $80 cost for printing the original photo would be returned.

In the ER case, they decided to devote their next "Finish Line" column to their hospital experience before LHE could question why they would go to a facility that had been the topic of an investigation by the paper. Their column focused on how two caring police officers brought Brett to the hospital and noted he got good treatment from doctors and nurses there. But they did not mince words when it came to the payment.

We thought the $1,000 charge seemed a bit steep so we called around to other area hospitals and described the services. The average charge at those facilities was in the $650 range. Why the difference? And what will be the charges for the doctor to remove the stitches in a few days?

They figured that Frank McDow or one of his fellow trustees might respond with a letter, but all of the comments on the website alluded to other patients who were unhappy with the costs of services they had at St. Mark's.

"More fodder for our case," said Harriet Lyman as she perused the communiques.

Christmas season arrived shortly thereafter and the festive decorations at their homes gave Janet and Kitty a bit of a respite from mulling over their legal problems. The annual Yuletide party of the Main Street Association always featured Santa Claus. For years, the role was handled by a barber whose physique matched that of the man from the North Pole. But the barber's untimely passing a few months prior to the holidays forced the business group to find a new Santa.

Ken Masterson volunteered.

"You're 6 feet, 7 inches tall," Kitty remarked to the advertising manager when he mentioned his new assignment. "Maybe the Jolly Green Giant but Santa?"

"Well, no one else volunteered and you want your kids to see Santa, right?"

Thus, Kitty and Janet and their five kids arrived at the VFW Hall where the party was held.

Eight-year-old Timmy McIntyre took one look at Ken the Santa and declared: "That is not Santa. Santa is a fat man. He is not a tall man."

The four Watson children appeared near tears with Marta noting loudly that "that is a false beard. Where is the real Santa?"

Janet and Kitty looked at each other as if to say "what do we tell these kids" when Ken, in his deep Santa voice, said calmly for all to hear: "I am Santa's helper from the North Pole. I came here today because Santa slipped and fell two days ago and had to go to the

North Pole Hospital to get stitches in his head. He is okay but cannot travel for a few days."

Then Ken turned to Brett Watson and said: "You fell and got stitches, correct? Santa told me about that. He wants to know how you are doing."

Brett and the others started to smile. The idea that the real Santa would know about Brett's injury convinced them that this substitute St. Nick had arrived right from the North Pole. They had no idea that Ken and the other Call staffers were well aware that their bosses had spent time in the ER with Brett.

One by one the children sat on Ken's lap and uttered lists of what they wanted for Christmas. Video games and dolls were high on the list. Then Molly Watson asked Santa what HE wanted for Christmas and Ken answered quickly as he looked at Kitty and Janet: "A raise."

"We hope your boss at the North Pole can swing it," said Janet. "Let us know if you get your wish."

She and Kitty laughed as they exited the holiday party.

"No matter what happens at work, we have these kids to keep us happy," said Janet.

CHAPTER 27

—

MARY QUINN, THE HIGHLY REGARDED libel lawyer, had appealed several times to the LHE attorneys to drop the defamation lawsuit against The Dunfield Call. She repeatedly was rebuffed and was convinced that the hospital corporation did not care about losing in a court trial. The objective was to put The Call out of business as a warning to other media outlets that LHE would not tolerate being the subject of investigative reporting.

In a meeting with Atty. Quinn, Kitty and Janet asked what chances The Call had in winning the lawsuit.

Quinn replied: "You and I know that your articles were truthful and well-edited with attribution," said Quinn. "But the jury has to understand that you are backed by laws that have existed since the 18th Century."

"Oh, yeah," said Janet. "Since 1735 as I recall. John Peter Zenger case."

"Wow, I am impressed," said Kitty. "How do you know that?"

"I actually got A in journalism history at Mizzou. I loved it."

"Well, we might be in journalism texts for this case," said Kitty. "Maybe for a media law class."

"I am more worried about being in the poor house," remarked Janet. "Our insurance policy monies have been spent and we are facing more legal and court costs. And if we lose, we could be hit with damages at a really high level. I find it hard to sleep at night as I try to figure this all out."

Janet, Kitty and Harriet, along with many friends, sat in the courtroom in the spring and listened as a lawyer representing Lerod Health Enterprises argued that LHE had been defamed in the articles published by The Call. He said that LHE was hurt financially as a result of the special section focusing on St. Mark's in Dunfield. He questioned a witness who worked on the LHE financial team; the witness said that fewer patients were being seen by doctors affiliated with LHE hospitals and that had affected the firm's bottom line.

Mary Quinn took exception the minute she stood up to rebut the LHE lawyer.

"The reason that you have fewer visits to doctors' offices is because you have fewer doctors! Physicians are flocking out of LHE, correct?"

The witness said he did not have any numbers to verify that.

Quinn walked to the table where she had been sitting and picked up a sheaf of papers.

"Well, I got the data in preparation for this case. In the past two years, you have lost at least 20 percent of the physicians at every hospital bought out by your company. Here are their names and I will bring some of them to this court if need be to tell why they are leaving. And believe me, it has nothing to do with articles in a small Connecticut weekly newspaper."

The LHE lawyers took to reading an editorial published in The Call's special section along with the other stories.

"It says that the care at St. Mark's is deteriorating and that is a ridiculous charge," said the lawyer.

Again, Mary Quinn was on top of the debate.

"An editorial is an opinion piece. Ditto for a column on the editorial page. Writers have a right to opinionate. By the way, your firm did not send a letter to the editor to refute those comments, did you? And please note that the owners of The Call wrote a Finish Line column about the good care one of their children got at St. Mark's after the articles in question were published. They did question the high cost of treatment and compared it to what the same type of treatment would have been at other Hartford area hospitals. That is called good reporting."

Emma Kloster proved to be a good witness as she described the unexpected passing of her spouse at St. Mark's. A few others who were quoted in the articles also took the witness stand and performed admirably. Megan McCarthy, who had quit her job at the New Jersey hospital owned by Lerod, described the difficult working conditions there and pointed to the back of the audience in the courtroom.

"Three other nurses who left the hospital drove up here with me today from Jersey. They know what I am talking about."

For four days, the back-and-forth continued. Area media outlets, including the Hartford Tribune and television stations, reported every day on the action. Kitty represented the owners on the witness stand and professionally and expertly described the reportorial process utilized in the investigative journalistic work. Quinn brought in two First Amendment specialists to boost her arguments about freedom of the press, as well as a highly touted law professor who could rattle off the results of other similar "David vs. Goliath" cases wherein a large company takes on a small business.

Quinn's closing argument to the jury was what Kitty called "brilliant" as it solidified the right of small newspapers to undertake serious investigative stories without the threat of forced closure because of the high cost of what she called "nuisance defamation cases---ones that a company knows it cannot win but undergoes simply to put the defendants out of business."

Convinced that his side would win, the LHE's main lawyer remarked to Kitty and Janet that he expected that his firm would reap hundreds of thousands of dollars in punitive damages.

"Good God," said Kitty. "Even if we win we have to come up with close to $300,000 for the lawyers' fees, and court cost, including payments and travel expenses for the high-powered witnesses. We will have to sell our souls."

Janet looked down at her shoes.

"I like these pumps. Not selling these soles."

Kitty chuckled.

"As I have always said, Janet, you should be a stand-up comedian."

As expected, the jury ruled in favor of The Call. Janet, Kitty and their spouses and friends erupted in cheers as the decision was rendered.

Off they all went to the nearby Dunfield Pub to celebrate the legal victory. Mary Quinn stood and said she was "overjoyed" to have had the opportunity to represent The Call. As she was speaking, her cell phone rang and she answered it. She seemed angry as she listened to the caller. She hung up and said: "Christ. That was Mr. Birge, the LHE lawyer, to tell me that they will be appealing the decision."

Kitty and Janet looked at each other and could hardly talk.

"We will have to close the paper. We cannot continue to fund this case, even though we did nothing wrong. Damn that Lerod company," said Janet.

"It is a ploy," said Quinn. "It will never go that far. My firm will handle it through dealing with Birge and the other Lerod lawyers."

Hank Watson, in a celebratory mood a moment before, looked green. Hank handled The Call's books and knew that, after the legal insurance monies had been expended for the trial, The Call could not afford another cent to cover additional costs.

"We cannot handle this," he said. "I think the paper should be sold and you can focus on expanding NEWScamp and your news syndicate."

You could see the disappointment in the faces of the many friends who a minute before had been high-fiving the victors.

"I will continue to pray," said Sister Louise Loftus, their high school friend who had shown up every day in court after ensuring them that she had been saying a daily rosary for months to support the pair whom she had helped in the fake canoe race two decades before.

CHAPTER 28

———

KITTY AND JANET FOUND THEIR business-related problems to be encompassing their mindsets. But as they weighed their options as to whether to sell the paper to cover the legal costs for the appeal, they vowed to maintain their normal lives as moms and professionals. That included spending time with their close friends from St. Aggies; one day several of them got together for lunch at Donegal Fields, an Irish pub and restaurant that had been a favorite haunt of theirs for years. Sister Louise Loftus was among the group and was downing a beer along with the others. She was teaching part-time at a local Catholic high school while attending law school at night.

"I cannot believe the order sent you to law school," said Kitty.

"Actually, it is a smart thing to do in the opinion of our superiors. I can eventually join our small legal staff and still continue to teach. More options is really the reason. We have two of our nursing nuns who are in medical school now. Another is getting her MBA at Harvard. Most of us get scholarships to cut down on the costs."

"You are the coolest nun, Lou" said Kitty, calling Sister Louise by the nickname she had since high school.

"One beer is my limit," laughed Lou. "If I returned to my convent in bad shape, I would be reported to Mother Superior and no doubt kicked right out of the order."

"At St. Agnes, I doubt if we ever had any nuns who imbibed," said Janet. "Well, maybe Adrienne."

She was referring to Sister Adrienne, the history teacher whom they all loved.

"Remember she made us memorize the Presidents. I can still do it."

"So can all of us, I think," added Penny Wilson, a classmate who had recently relocated from New York after her spouse took a top post at an insurance firm. As she said this, the group broke into the chant: "Washington, Adams, Jefferson, Madison, Monroe" as they whisked through the names of the nation's chief executives. "Cleveland, Harrison, Cleveland, again," they shouted as they hit the end of the 19th Century and emphasized that Grover Cleveland had two non-successive terms in the White House.

"I loved how Sister Adrienne taught and also how she led the singing on the bus as we headed to a museum or a basketball game," said Kitty. "Where is she now, Lou?"

"She is a prayer minister in our retirement residence in Hartford," said Sister Louise.

"You mean the old nuns' home," said Janet. "That is what we always called it. You have gotten a bit high falutin' with your language since you joined the convent."

"Well, it really is a nursing home but our order assigns the nuns there to be so-called prayer ministers who are supposed to be praying for everyone in the world, but basically they are receiving the best care possible after their years of teaching or nursing. And even elderly mothers of nuns are allowed to live there. Sister

Adrienne, who is only in her 70s and sharp as a tack, is at The Villa because she is fighting Parkinsons and needs medical care. I visit her a lot and also periodically help St. Agnes Academy Alumnae Association with running the weekly Bingo games. Haven't you all helped with that over the years?"

In concert, her friends said "No."

She explained that each week a number of volunteers from a particular graduating class help out, and that their class from more than 20 years ago was booked the coming week to handle the Bingo.

"I am supposed to round up some classmates, so I am recruiting you guys. Next Monday---or Bingo Monday as we call it."

Still guilty that they embarrassed their families with the fake canoe race, Kitty and Janet always felt they owed the sisters something for the good education they received, and regularly donated to the annual fund to pay for expenses for the nuns at the retirement facility.

"OK. It sounds like fun and we are covered at the office then, so Janet and I will be there," said Kitty.

"Darn right," laughed Janet, who boasted about the Bingo games she called for relatives every year at her aunt's Thanksgiving dinner. "Frankly, I love Bingo!"

Sister Louise explained that the volunteers usually bring prizes, "like perfume or writing paper or linen handkerchiefs or candy or flowers. And one person calls the numbers while the rest of us, along with some nurses and other volunteers, help the nuns with their Bingo cards. And the nuns really look forward to it. You know, their average age is 89. Nuns live long."

"Maybe because you don't have to put up with operating a newspaper company," said Kitty.

"And dumb lawsuits," added Janet.

Lou reminded them that sisters in her order prayed for Janet and Kitty during the libel trial.

Janet, Kitty, Penny, Lou and a few other classmates arrived on "Bingo Monday" at the Blessed Mother Villa, home to the retired nuns near the Motherhouse of the Sisters of St. Sebastian. They walked into a room filled with retired nuns, in the traditional habits that the younger nuns never donned; some elderly mothers of nuns, and nurses/volunteers ready to help out. Janet was assigned to be the Bingo caller after Sister Lou told the Villa supervisor that "my friend here is a veteran numbers' caller."

Things were going well until Janet tried to be funny as she often did.

"Carpe Diem, Sisters. You know what that means: Seize the day!"

"We all know Latin, honey," remarked a stern-faced nun in her original habit.

"I know that," said Janet. "For me at St. Aggies it was Veni, Vidi, Evacui. I came, I saw, I got the heck out."

"You are NOT funny," yelled the same nun. "Just call the numbers."

A few minutes later, Sister Louise came to the front and whispered to Janet: "Recognize her? The one who does not appreciate your good humor?"

"No. They all look alike in those outfits, Lou."

"Sister Margaret Anne."

"Oh, Christ," said Janet. "THE Sister Margaret Anne as in the directress who nailed us for the fake canoe bit?"

"Yep, and she still cannot believe I am a nun."

They looked over at Sister Adrienne, who actually was laughing at the Latin exchange. No doubt she was still reeling from her years of working for the domineering Sister Margaret Anne.

After a number of Bingo games were finished, Lou quietly told Janet that they would now go into winner mode.

"What?" asked Janet, who was enjoying her stint as Bingo caller.

"We want to make sure all of the residents win a prize so you need to call out the numbers needed by those who have not yet won," said Sister Louise quietly. "So I will look around during the next few games and give you signals about numbers and then you call them."

"This should be a paid job," Janet uttered loudly enough for Sister Margaret Anne to remark: "You think you are good or something?"

The Bingo calling started again and Janet saw Sister Lou in the back, looking over the shoulder of a 100-year-old nun who had not yet won a game. Then Lou raised her arm in the air and "drew" the letter B followed by her raising two fingers.

Janet got the message. She pulled the next number from a rotating wheel and it was "O 73." But she yelled "B2" instead and the centenarian sister weakly and happily said "BINGO."

This deceitful way to play Bingo continued with Janet following in-the-air instructions until the final game, when Lou noticed that a sister needed "O69" and tried to convey that by opening her fingers ten at a time. Janet thought she got the message, pulled "N35" and said "O68." She was off by one, and a sister who already had two prizes yelled "BINGO" again. Janet felt bad that she had misconstrued the message. But Sister Lou saved the day. She came to the front and announced that all of the residents had won prizes except one nun, so she is "our lucky winner of the day for bucking the odds and being the lone non-winner. So, Sister Madeline, you get the big prize, a lovely bouquet of flowers that will be delivered to your room tomorrow. Courtesy of members of our St. Agnes Academy class who are here today."

The wheelchair-bound Sister Madeline said she was "thrilled" as others in the room applauded her good luck.

As the Villa staff escorted the retired nuns out of the room, Sister Louise turned to the volunteers and said: "Now we need to cough up some cash for those flowers I just decided to send."

"Covered," laughed Janet. "Studer Florist is one of our advertisers and we will double the size of their ad next time for a beautiful bouquet sent here for Sister Madeline. Now let's head to lunch. I need sustenance after that gig."

"You were really good," said Kitty. "You really are a Call girl."

The following day, Kitty and Janet weighed the possibility of writing their next "Finish Line" column about their foray into what Janet called "Cheatin' Bingo at the Nunnery."

"It might be a comedic movie but I do not think Sister Louise and the other nuns of St. Sebastian would look kindly about our revelation that the weekly games are rigged to ensure 100 percent winners," responded Kitty.

They had the office staff laughing heartily as they described the Bingo Day and directed Ken Masterson to double the size of the flower shop's ad in return for a large bouquet sent to the Villa for Sister Madeline.

In the end, though, they did decide to write that week's "Finish Line" column about the retired nuns as an entrée into slamming the plan by LHE to close the nursing home affiliated for years with St. Mark's.

So if you want to know how best to treat elders needing nursing care, just look to the Blessed Mother Villa operated by the Sisters of St. Sebastian for their retired nuns and for some of the sisters' elderly mothers.

We went there last week and discovered that a wonderful staff oversees the job of ensuring that the residents get superb, loving care. Most of these nuns (average age is 89) have no other family members, so their late-in-the-game lifestyles are in the hands of smiling nurses and volunteers who help with many of the activities. The adequately furnished facility, with private rooms for the residents, depends on donations from many fronts. Those of us who have had the opportunity to learn in the Sebastian schools like our alma mater, St. Agnes Academy, try to donate regularly for the upkeep of the Villa. Many ex-students also give their time in reading to those whose vision is hampered or taking care of the lovely chapel where the nuns attend Mass or even overseeing the weekly, popular Bingo games.

We would not even try to compare it to the nursing home run by Lerod Health Enterprises, owner of St. Mark's. After all, what we know about the current operation there is hearsay because we are not allowed to step foot inside the place, even to visit a resident who formerly rented an apartment we own in The Dunfield Call building. Our investigative report, supported by a recent jury decision in our favor, has made us unwelcome at the nursing home. But insiders, including those with relatives at the facility, tell us that things have changed over the past few years with staff members laid off and private rooms now housing two patients. We and others in Dunfield rue the plans for the home's closing and want it to return to its once-beloved state.

The copy was correct as it was printed, but only because super copy editor Kitty caught a typo just before the paper was to be sent to the printer.

"Oh, my God," she exclaimed as she read over the column. "In the first sentence, it should be **nursing** care, not **cursing** care."

"Thank God you caught that," said Janet who had typed the column, "or we probably would have our St. Aggies diplomas rescinded by the nuns!"

CHAPTER 29

———

JANET'S SPORTSWRITING BACKGROUND WAS IN evidence as she helped to strengthen the writing of a few UConn interns who were covering some of the local sports events. Of particular interest in Fall was the Dunfield High football team that was undefeated for the first time in years. Janet assigned two sports-minded interns to cover football and other fall sports at the high school.

With enthusiasm mounting around town for an upcoming weekend game against nemesis Clayhill High School, one intern, Dan, went to the high school field to write a pre-game report. He returned to The Call offices with some news.

"I had hoped to speak to the quarterback but when I asked an assistant coach about him, I was ushered off the field. I could see the other players looking sort of dejected but no one would talk to me."

Janet was puzzled. When The Call first opened, the school system's PR person, Maria Watkins, was contentious and operated as a gatekeeper to all school personnel. But she had eased up over the years as the paper had published much positive material about the local schools. And the interns had interviewed players in recent weeks at practices without being unceremoniously removed from the football field.

"Let me get on this, Dan," she said.

A call to Watkins produced no information. At first, Janet thought Maria might be hiding something, but the latter seemed surprised that the intern would not have access to the field as The Call's writers had been welcomed to high school team practices and had written credible stories about the teams and athletes. Maria Watkins apparently made a call to the football coach who merely informed her that the quarterback was not at practice this week. That is all he would tell the PR head, and she called Janet at the paper with that information.

"There is a story here," said Janet to Maria. "And if you can't get it, I will."

Janet phoned Harriet Lyman, whose stepson Adam was on the staff of the Dunfield High newspaper. Harriet said she would ask Adam if he knew what might be going on with the football team.

With Harriet's prodding, Adam had attended a summer NEWScamp for students and had gained a love of journalistic work. He proved to be a good source for The Call as he discovered, through hearing conversations at the high school, that the star quarterback had been hospitalized after a drug overdose.

"So I guess he is off the team," Harriet told Janet and Kitty, "just as Dunfield goes into the state playoffs."

Adam and his fellow high school reporters then found out, by asking questions of a few football players whom they knew, that three other players quietly were thrown off the team earlier in the season when the coaches discovered they were taking illegal drugs. They remained as students and nothing was said around the school about the trio.

"Seems as if the football guys agreed to keep quiet about this drug stuff," Adam said. "But after the quarterback's overdose, some of the players were angry about such shenanigans and are willing to talk anonymously to our reporters. We wanted to write a story for this week's school paper but our adviser said the article would never pass muster with the principal."

"Damn that Hazelwood," said Kitty.

"I agree," said Janet, as the two referred to a famous legal case that gave high school principals the right to stop the publication of a paper that included something they did not like to see in print.

But The Dunfield Call had no such restrictions, so Janet accompanied intern Dan to the football field the next day. She approached the coach and introduced herself. Immediately he turned away while mumbling "No comment."

But she had not asked a question.

"No comment on what?" she asked.

He continued walking toward the school building while motioning for team members to follow him to the locker rooms. Dan snapped pictures of the team's movements while Janet followed the coach and said: "What is it that you will not comment on? And is your starting quarterback ready for this week's game?"

A few players snickered when she asked that but they kept walking with their teammates into the high school building.

Janet and Dan tried to enter the high school but were stopped by the coach who said: "You cannot come in here."

Janet returned to her office and phoned Maria Watkins.

"Ok," said Janet. "Your football coach apparently is hiding something. We know through sources that the quarterback is in a rehab place and earlier this year a few other players were bounced from the team for drug use. It appears that this information is being kept from you, the superintendent, and the board. Or, if not, certainly you all are keeping it from the town residents. And the coach thinks he has the right to keep us out of the building. Hey, maybe the school has a rule that we have to sign in or something, but he slammed the door in our faces. We are going to write a story about this whole situation."

Maria Watkins said little but mentioned that she was not thrilled that the paper would publish a story "that could hurt our students."

Janet was a bit miffed. She wanted to give Maria a lesson in journalistic ethics but she saved the discussion for Kitty, who walked into the office while Janet was on the phone with the schools' PR person.

"Kits, wait until you hear this. Dan and I were bounced out of the high school after the coach refused to speak to us. It is clear there is a drug problem on that team, and Adam Lyman is getting more information through sources there. Of course, the school bigwigs, who apparently are just learning about this, want us to keep quiet so we won't hurt the kids."

"It might be trouble, but we are going to publish a story, correct?" asked Kitty.

"Of course, and for good reason," answered Janet.

Then Janet turned to Dan and another intern seated nearby.

"Do you two understand the relationship of philosophy to journalism?"

Neither answered.

"For one thing," said Janet, "philosophers and reporters both ask questions so we see some professional ties therein. More importantly, some philosophers have ideas that can be used in our field. Take John Stuart Mill and his utilitarianism: the greatest good for the greatest number. Move that philosophy into media ethics and decision-making in the newsroom. Right now should we forget about what we know about the town's beloved football team and add to what appears to be a cover-up just to keep the schools' good reputation intact, or would the greatest good be for the town newspaper to inform the taxpayers and parents of students that there appears to be a problem that might extend beyond the team?"

Kitty applauded her partner: "Boy, you really did learn at Mizzou."

"Yes," said Janet, "and that is why I got to grad school in communication and decided to write my master's thesis on philosophy and journalism. Want to know about Immanuel Kant?"

"Kant? Can't say I do," laughed Kitty. "But you made your point and let's get to work on the story. My editing pen is ready to go."

Janet explained to the interns that she would put the story together with their help and from information from their main source, Adam Lyman, who would not be named. The story would go in without a byline, she said, "so that if trouble arises, you interns will not be involved." She said that the story would not name the quarterback because no public information had been acknowledged about his status. But she reminded the others, that when that star player is not on the field for the upcoming playoff game, townspeople would figure out the person pretty quickly. She also had been given the names of those kicked off the team for drug use---Adam got that information from his football team sources---but nothing would be verified by Maria Watkins or any official person in the school district.

"The bad thing for us is that no one will go on record---not the coach, the school superintendent, no one. I hate to publish a story that lacks such depth, but it still is an important article."

So, when the next edition of The Dunfield Call, came out, the bottom of the front page featured a headline, created by Kitty, that merely asked: **Drug Problems on the Gridiron?**

Early in the football season, at least three players were removed from the Dunfield High team after it was discovered they were taking illegal drugs, according to sources.

The revelation was made anonymously by other students at the school after questions were raised earlier this week about another player having suffered a drug overdose that required his admittance to a rehab center.

When two Call reporters went to the high school field to seek information as to the validity of the reports, they were met with a "No Comment" remark from Coach Bill Shannon, who then had the pair removed from the school building. The Dunfield School Board of Education's community affairs director, Maria Watkins, said Monday that she was unaware of students being removed from the team, or of any player who had suffered a drug overdose. She said she would check with Coach Shannon to see why he refused to allow reporters into a public building. So far, we have had no response with that information.

Sources on the football team said that, after the second week of practice, Coach Shannon told players that he was upset to discover that some team members were taking illegal drugs and that he had removed a few from the team. He warned the others that they would face removal also if he learned about their taking anything deemed illegal. He also said that "next time" he would report the students to school district officials, thus giving the impression that no report was made about the three players who were thrown off the team.

When contacted by The Call, Pam Dillon, president of the high school Parents' Organization, said that over the past weekend she heard through the grapevine that a student on the football team had been sent for rehabilitation, but made it clear that "it was a rumor. I have no idea about the truth of it." She did confirm that she had called for the group's executive board to meet tonight to "quell rumors or to figure out what is happening."

The football team also has a parents' group that helps with providing pre-game meals and transportation, but phone messages left by the paper to some of those parents went unreturned.

Jack Johnston, a physician who has volunteered for more than a decade as the team doctor, also refused to answer questions, saying that "you have to speak to Miller." He was referring to Dr. Fred Miller, the Dunfield schools superintendent. To interview him requires that reporters make a request to Watkins, who said Miller had no comment about questions relating to the team.

Dunfield High will host Clayhill High at 7 p.m. Friday in the first round of District 3 state playoffs. As of Wednesday morning, the team's printed roster on the schools' website remains the same as it has for the past several weeks, and includes the name of the player who sources on the team say is now at a rehabilitation center out of state.

Psychologist Mary Anne Munley, who heads the Family Center in Dunfield and writes a monthly column carried in The Call, said she is seeing an increase in the number of local families dealing with drug issues among teenagers. She stressed that she has no knowledge about the football team and drug use.

Kitty and Janet perused the paper after copies had arrived in their office from the printer.

"How long do you think it will be before the phone rings?" asked Kitty.

"Let's see," answered Janet. "The papers will not arrive through the mail for subscribers until tomorrow, but they are for sale at the local stores and we have the online edition already up. So I say maybe two hours before administrators or parents start complaining that we are hurting Dunfield by publishing such stuff."

"So what should we say to these people, Janet?"

"Kitty, we just say: Utilitarianism."

They laughed just as the phone rang. It was not a Dunfield complainant but Ken Masterson on the cell phone he used to keep in touch with advertisers.

"I just got a call from Kline's, the biggest advertiser in our paper. Their ad guy said to cancel all future advertisements."

"Klines?" asked Janet and Kitty together as they listened on a speaker phone. "Why?"

"I do not know any specifics but the ad guy said it had something to do with Mr. Rafter. He's the owner of Kline's, right?"

"Yes," said Kitty, "He lives in Dunfield and started advertising soon after we started because he liked what we were doing in the town."

"Wait a minute," said Janet. "Rafter? Oh God, the quarterback's name---one we did not print because we did not have official confirmation--- is Kyle Rafter."

"Well," added Kitty "The greatest good for the town was not the greatest for us!"

CHAPTER 30

—

ONE DAY, AFTER FINISHING HER "Oh, Mother" column, Janet stood up and yawned.

"This mother is tired of writing and working. I think I should take the kids to the movies."

"How about the circus?" asked Clara. "You can get free tickets if you write a review."

Turns out Clara had received a call from a public relations staffer for a circus coming to Hartford for a week. The circus employee was seeking to have reviews of the performances and offered free tickets to media representatives.

"That's us. Media mavens," said Janet. "But we prefer paid ads."

"Won't happen," said Ken Masterson. "That circus will only advertise in The Tribune and on local TV, not in the small papers"

"Forget the free tickets," said Janet. "I consider that payola. Clara, tell that PR person that we are going to buy seven tickets for the Saturday matinee. Let her know that we pay our own way."

With the four Watson kids and Timmy McIntyre, Janet and Kitty arrived early at the circus tent set up in a mostly unused football field.

"I wonder if they sell chameleons," said Kitty. "My mother always talked about buying them at a circus in the 1950s."

"What is a chameleon anyway?" asked Janet as the children looked on with puzzled faces.

"I think it is a lizard," said Kitty, who took out her phone to look up the definition.

"I want a lizard," said Timmy as the Watson quartet agreed in unison.

Kitty then announced that her search revealed that chameleons are a "specialized clade of old World lizards."

"Can we get a clade?" asked Molly.

Janet threw up her hands and declared that "I don't even know what a clade is let alone a chameleon. Forget it. There are no lizards for sale here. But we need to get those great circus peanuts so we can throw the shells on the floor. That is what I love about the circus."

The got to their seats as a forlorn-looking clown peddling his wares came near to their section. He was yelling "popcorn, candy, soda."

"Peanuts, please," implored Janet.

"Sorry, lady. No peanuts at the circus."

"What?" said Kitty. "You don't sell peanuts? At a circus?"

"No," said the clown. "Not since the anti-peanut people complained to the bigwigs at the home office."

"For real? No peanuts?" asked Janet.

"Something about kids being allergic to peanuts," said the clown as he shook his head.

They reluctantly settled for popcorn just as the ringmaster called for the beginning of a parade of circus performers. Included was a small car, driven by clowns and filled with colorfully dressed dogs and a slew of kittens.

"Marta is allergic to cats, right, Janet?" asked Kitty.

"Yes indeed. She gets shots for that. But an anti-cat group? Never heard of that. They have lots of cats at the circus!"

In unison, Kitty and Janet sang out: "Our next column!"

And indeed their next "Finish Line" column borrowed from their experience at the circus:

"Peanuts. Popcorn. Soda."

If you have been to a circus, you know how often a clown comes by pleading for the audience to shell out some bucks for those snacks.

Oops, that word SHELL was out of favor at the circus we attended a few days ago in Hartford. We were looking forward to treating our children to bags of peanuts in shells. We have always loved eating those peanuts and then throwing the shells on the dirt floor of the Big Top.

Turns out the circus has gone peanut-less.

Credit that move to a group of people whose offspring reportedly have allergies to peanuts.

Jennifer Morris, the circus' PR person, said threats of boycotts started more than a year ago from groups of parents of children with allergies to peanuts. After realizing the potential economic implications, the circus executives cut out sales of peanuts altogether.

So NO ONE gets to throw those peanut shells on the circus floor.

Oh, and no elephants either in the ring. The animal rights people got involved and the circus removed the elephants from the performances.

And yet the acrobatic family from Eastern Europe has its teenagers flying through the air or shot out of cannons. No threats from the family safety advocates.

Heck, if you were a real health nut who watches every morsel you eat, would you really take your kids to see the Fat Lady at the circus?

Despite our reservations, our kids really enjoyed the circus. We adults were the ones who were scared to watch those trapeze artists. We could not even look up at them as our kids laughed at us. Maybe we need to see a psychologist to ease our fears.

Hope he serves peanuts.

As expected, the paper received several nasty letters from parents of children with peanut allergies and one from a pediatrician who acknowledged that peanut allergies are serious but "that should not force the circus to eliminate selling the popular treat. Parents of allergic children should be vigilant regarding their own off-spring without ruining the experience of others."

"This letter will make it to print," said Kitty as she read it out loud as she munched on a bag of salted peanuts.

CHAPTER 31

———

GOING TO THE CIRCUS OR doing all of the Mommy-led routines provided a diversion of sorts for Kitty and Janet, as they continued to engage in good journalistic practices.

"We are watchdogs, as they say in our profession," said Kitty. "We do not shy away from letting readers know what is happening, even if it is tough for us to do so."

The initial article about the football team was followed up by a few others about meetings that ensued after the news about the drugs got out. Some parents at the high school called for the ouster of the football coach who had failed to tell school administrators that he had removed players early in the season after learning they were taking illegal drugs, reportedly to beef up their teenage bodies. Meetings with the School Board were packed with people railing on either for or against the coach. The Rafters, parents of the quarterback, sat silently through one meeting, but at the next one called for the ouster of the coach, arguing that had they known that players were taking illegal drugs they might have been aware of their son's problems.

"And," said Ken Rafter, "don't think my son is the only Dunfield High student at the rehab center where he is recovering. It is not just athletes."

That remark seemed to shock the assemblage, according to Harriet, who was covering the meeting for The Call.

In the end, the coach was fired, a drug counselor was added to the high school staff, and a town police officer was assigned fulltime to the school. In addition, the Parents' Association scheduled a lecture by one of the nation's foremost authorities on teens and drugs; the auditorium was "packed," as Harriet wrote in her article about the event.

Janet and Kitty also wrote a brief editorial that praised the town for its reaction to the news originally spread by The Call:

Dunfield citizens deserve a pat on the back for their quick response to reports that drugs might be infiltrating the high school. The School Board listened to scores of townspeople with an opinion on the issue, and was correct in removing Coach Bill Shannon from the football team staff.

Whether he should remain as a history teacher is a matter for the board to decide. But his unwillingness to reveal drug problems on his team, and his attempt to keep media from the DHS building clearly show that he is not able to handle the responsibilities that go along with being a high school coach and mentor.

We want to salute the Rafters, parents of the football player who is in rehab after a drug overdose. They stepped up to the plate in a public forum and warned other parents that the problem extends past the football team. Now the school board, the Parents' Organization and the police are among groups taking steps to deal with any drug-related problems.

Good for Dunfield!

"Even though it cost us quite a bit with the loss of Kline's advertising, we still need to use our editorial clout to support this town," said Kitty as she checked the editorial and other stories for the week's issue.

"Well, with the libel appeal and everything else, we could be costing ourselves right out of business," said Janet.

LHE's appeal of the libel decision was dragging out, and lawyer Mary Quinn was keeping on top of it---at a heavy cost for The Call owners. After months of waiting, lawyer Quinn got to read the extensive material provided to the appeals court by Lerod Health Enterprises. She was astounded that the LHE attorneys argued that the jury that ruled in The Call's favor was "biased" because most jurors lived in towns where people support weekly papers or they were types who did not like hospitals at all.

"As my dear Irish dad would say, it is a lot of shenanigans, a lot of hooey," said Quinn, who set about to write a lengthy response to the Lerod argument.

"Cripes, why is it so darn expensive for legal fees?" asked Kitty. "Maybe we should investigate legal firms."

"Don't even go there," said Janet as they sipped Chardonnay at their weekly business meeting a few weeks after Christmas. "We have enough trouble as it is. Hank is getting really upset as he checks the books every week. We may have to get out of this business."

They half-heartedly discussed how their side businesses might fare if they sold the newspaper. NEWScamp was a hit, for sure, but the revenue stream was limited because parents were reluctant to pay more than a certain fee for workshops for their children, be it in journalism or any out-of-school activity. Their syndicate now handled 10 columnists who wrote on varied topics, from nutrition to bridge, but many newspapers in the nation were slashing their columns to save money and publishing free blogs and other materials.

Janet's own "Oh, Mother" column was affected when a number of newspapers carrying it were forced to shut their doors. The Call owners did get income from renters in two small apartments in the building, but no doubt the structure would be sold along with the newspaper business if the pair decided on giving up the ship.

"What bothers me most," said Kitty, "is that the paper is successful in itself. We have enough ads to cover our costs, and still generate some decent money for us. That is, without dealing with lawsuits like that hospital one."

The phone rang and Janet answered it. She was surprised that it was a call from Mike Collins, the managing editor of The Hartford Tribune. As a Dunfield resident, he was a regular reader of The Call and a frequent golf partner of Hank Watson and Tim McIntyre. At his behest, the Tribune covered the LHE vs. The Dunfield Call trial and, at the time, he had published a strong editorial that supported the "great journalism exhibited in the work of a small-town paper."

"Hi, Mike," said Janet. "What's up?"

"I think you should be entered into the Pulitzer Prize competition."

"What?" said Janet as she hit the speaker button on the phone so Kitty could hear the conversation.

Collins said he and others in the newspaper business felt the work of The Dunfield Call deserved recognition and wanted to assist by helping put in an entry for the Pulitzer Prize in local reporting.

"We will need documentation, including copies of all of the articles related to the hospital investigation."

"Wow," said Kitty. "Nominated for a Pulitzer."

Collins pointed out that many entries are sent to the Pulitzer committee, and only a few move on to nominee status and consideration for the prestigious journalism award.

"Oh, well, just being mentioned in the same conversation as Joseph Pulitzer is enough for me," said Janet.

She assigned Clara to get the materials together and thanked Michael Collins for being so supportive.

The latest legal bills for Mary Quinn's firm sent Janet and Kitty into a headspin.

"We try to do something good with the Lerod stories and it costs us a darn fortune," said Janet. "I don't want to show this bill to Hank or he might call a real estate agent today. I think we are insolvent."

"Insolvent," remarked Kitty. "How about **in-trouble**? And yet our work is being entered into a national competition? Amazing."

The pair was infuriated that LHE was bankrolling a legal appeal just to make a point that it could knock a small business to oblivion.

Clara strode into the office to tell them she had received a phone call that Mrs. Rockwell, the wealthy nose-in-the-air widow and former owner of The Call, had passed away in Palm Beach.

"I worked for her husband and while the paper was not as good as it is now, he and his wife were most kind to me. I am saddened by her death."

Mrs. Rockwell's obit ran on The Call's front page and noted that her funeral service would be at Dunfield Presbyterian Church. Kitty convinced Janet that "it would be nice if we went as representatives of the re-invented Call."

"Wow---a Catholic trying to get me, the Protestant, to go to a Protestant church. All right."

The service, attended by about 50 friends and relatives, was solemn but touching as the deceased's son, Jared, spoke about how his mother and his late father had helped many people through their Rockwell Foundation. He also said that after his mother sold The Call to its current owners, she subscribed to the paper and "read every word of it each week as soon as it came in the mail. She so enjoyed reading it."

Sitting in a pew in the back of the church, Janet and Kitty both smiled.

Later, at a repast in the church hall, Janet said to Kitty: "I never thought that a Rockwell would speak kindly about our venture."

They thanked Jared for his gracious remark and he told them that his mother was "incensed that Lerod Health Enterprises would take you on and figured it might bankrupt you."

"Unfortunately, she could be right, Jared," said Kitty. "We may have to sell out."

A week later, a call from Mary Quinn floored The Call staff.

"LHE dropped the appeal," she said. "Think they realized you would win and decided to avoid any more bad publicity. Believe me, the jury decision was going to be upheld."

Janet and Kitty were relieved---to a point.

"One monkey off our back, as they say," said Kitty.

"But," emphasized Janet, "in a sense, Lerod won anyway. Hank says we have to sell the paper to cover the legal costs. Heck, we have not even received Mary Quinn's final bill and we have no idea how many hours her firm worked on the response to the appeal."

"Can we swing a loan?" asked Kitty.

"You want more debt? Seriously, Kits, is that what we need? All I think about these days is how we can sustain our business. But we have another business---called motherhood---and I want to rid my mind of the financial headaches and get on with other things. It would be different if we did not have this debt hanging over our heads. And exactly where would we get a loan? Even Hank's bank would turn us down; after all we have a heavy debt load now. All because of a lawsuit. You know even if we were to ignore our lawyers' recommendations and go ahead and sue Lerod to pay our legal fees, we could not pay lawyers to handle our case! Talk about a lousy situation."

CHAPTER 32

———

EASTER SUNDAY COINCIDED WITH AN annual ritual started years before by Kitty's late mom: planting the magic beans.

Children in the extended Moran family would be given "magic" beans supplied by Mrs. Moran. On Holy Saturday, the day before Easter, they would plant those beans outside their homes. Then, on Easter morning, the children would return to the planting sites and *Voila*: the beans had sprouted lollipops.

"Are we on for the magic beans this year?" asked Janet, who had joined Kitty in overseeing the yearly Easter plantings and whose children looked forward to it.

"Yes, of course," said Kitty, "and I think we have 10 families to cover this year."

When Janet and Kitty would explain the annual undertaking, friends would say they wanted in, so The Call owners would add them to the list.

That meant getting more "magic beans." So off they would go to the supermarket and purchase navy beans that they told the children were "magic beans" that they had been given by a secret friend. The children never asked who the friend might be so, as Kitty said, "we never had to deal with that."

As in the past years, the beans were put into individual plastic bags. On Holy Saturday afternoon, Timmy McIntyre and the

Watson children joined their mothers as they drove to various homes and distributed the bags to young friends who planted the beans in their yards, as did the Watsons and Timmy in their respective front yards.

That night, when their children were asleep, Kitty and Janet exited their respective abodes with hundreds of lollipops that they had ordered online. Looking like burglars in their dark clothing, they crawled onto the lawns of the homes where the magic beans had been planted and stuck lollipops in the ground.

(They had experienced pretty much smooth sailing every year, except for the time that a neighbor's youngster woke up, looked out the window and saw the women on their knees in the yard. He screamed for his parents, who calmed the boy down, returned him to bed, and came to the front door with two beers for their friends, Kitty and Janet.)

"These are beautiful lollipops," said Janet as she planted a bunch in the yard of the home of their friend, Penny Wilson. "Glad we can still afford them!"

"Well, this is so much fun for the kids," said Kitty. "I know when I was young I always awoke on Easter to see if the magic beans had sprouted lollipops."

As they crawled near the front porch to continue placing the lollipops, they saw a car with flashing lights turn into the Wilsons' driveway.

"A police car? Something wrong at the Wilsons?" said Kitty to Janet.

"From the looks on the faces of the cop coming across the lawn, I think there is something wrong with us Call Girls!" answered her partner.

When the officer flashed a light into her face, Janet said: "Are you on the lollipop unit tonight?"

The policeman was not amused.

"What are you up to?" he asked the two newspaperwomen.

"Just planting some lollipops," answered Kitty.

"Well, see," said Janet, "the Wilson kids in this house planted magic beans here today and now we are planting lollipops."

"What? Are you two making this up? This is not your property, correct?" said the cop.

"No. We are just here to plant lollipops," remarked Janet.

The policeman did not crack a smile, but Janet and Kitty looked at each other and burst out laughing.

"Why are you laughing?" asked the officer.

"Because this will make a good story," chuckled Janet.

"What? That you were caught trespassing?"

"This is the home of our friend, Penny Wilson. Ask her if we are trespassing."

"Janet, I think Penny said the family was going to her in-laws for some sort of party tonight," said Kitty.

"Well, trust me," said Janet to the officer. "We are here at the invitation of the Wilsons. Why do you think we are here? To rob the house or something??"

"You mean burglarize the house, Janet. We don't have guns," said Kitty, the competent copy editor who knew the difference between burglary and robbery.

"I have no idea what you are talking about, but you can explain it all at the station," said the policeman.

"Are we going to be arrested? For lollipop planting? This is front-page news," said Janet.

"Really," said the officer sarcastically. "I doubt if any reporter will ask me to describe this crazy case."

"Oh, and that quote will be high up in the story," said Janet as she and Kitty got into the back of the police car. "You did say crazy, correct?"

Sure enough, the next "Finish Line" column was headlined "Dunfield's Lollipop Caper."

Janet and Kitty first described their "Magic Beans" ritual and how they had been conducting the lollipop planting when they were interrupted and brought to the police station after the officer told them it was a "crazy" case. Then they wrote:

We sat in the back seat of the police car and made a cell phone call to Penny Wilson, whom we convinced to leave her family event and get to the station to verify that we had not trespassed on her property. We asked her to call Harriet Lyman, one of our part-time staffers and tell her to come down to cover the story.

At the station, we produced our licenses that showed we were Dunfield residents. Our names apparently did not ring a bell with the dispatcher or the several policemen in the office. Guess they do not read the town paper!

Anyway, we explained again that we were merely planting lollipops and they all looked at us as if we had ingested too much sugar.

When Penny arrived, she told the police that she was more than happy to have us on her property and that she loved the "magic bean" concept. The reaction of the officers showed that they might have added her to the crazy list. (Frankly, she was laughing at us).

Then came Harriet, our stalwart reporter who is also a lawyer. She asked why the owners of The Dunfield Call were being held and what, if any, charges were forthcoming.

"You two own the paper?" asked the officer who had discovered us in the Wilsons' yard.

"For more than four years now," said Janet. "But this will mark the first time that the town crime report might have our

names. *After all, we believe in transparency and accurate reporting.*"

We heard the dispatcher call the police chief at home. We know Chief Stephen Hazelle as we have interviewed him a number of times. Within about 10 minutes he walked into the station to find us, our friend Penny and our reporter Harriet all sucking on lollipops. Hazelle took the "arresting" officer into a back room and emerged a few minutes later.

"Sorry. A mistake. No charges."

No kidding.

Are we upset?

No. At least we know the Dunfield police are looking out for the properties and people in town.

But we are sure they were a bit surprised to see the hundreds of lollipops growing in front of the station on Easter morning. (See the photo on page 6).

CHAPTER 33

———

THE PULITZER PRIZE COMMITTEE ANNOUNCES finalists and winners on the same day. So newspapers or individuals who have been nominated usually wait in their respective newsrooms to hear the noon announcement.

Thus Janet and Kitty, along with their spouses, joined The Call staffers and a few friends in the newsroom and awaited the revelation of the winners' names. As the noon hour approached, they were taking bets.

"I think we are going to win," said Harriet as the others sort of chuckled.

"I'm betting the Local Reporting prize goes to the Kansas paper that covered the tornado," said Kitty, "although I have been praying that we could at least be named as a finalist."

"I thought I had the prayers covered," said Sister Louse, who had arrived to await the news.

Just in case, the champagne was being chilled in ice buckets and the owners of The Farmers' Bistro had been alerted that a celebration might be in order later.

Michael Collins arrived with a reporter and photographer from The Hartford Tribune.

"We want to take your picture even if you just make it to finalist status, and you should," said Collins. "It is an honor no matter what."

Hank Watson and Tim McIntyre huddled in the corner. Their names were on the contract as owners of the paper and were hoping that their wives' hard work would be recognized.

As newspaper staffs all over the country watched by videoconferencing, the finalists and winners' names were being called. Everything turned quiet at The Call as categories like International News and Photography were ticked off.

And then it came for the Local Reporting category. The finalists were named: A daily in North Dakota for coverage of regional transportation problems, and a reporter from a Texas for a series on droughts.

The group at The Call looked a bit dejected until the next announcement: **And The Pulitzer Prize for Local Reporting goes to The Dunfield Call for its investigation of the operation and ownership of a local hospital.**

The celebration began. The cheers could be heard down Main Street in Dunfield. Within minutes, the Famers' Bistro staff was arriving with plates of food. Merchants from local stores poured into the newspaper offices. Janet and Kitty were being hugged by everyone, and were saluting Harriet, who handled the bulk of the investigation, and Clara, who contributed so much to the layout of the special section. Michael Collins was lifting a glass of champagne and toasting the newly named Pulitzer recipients as his photographer took a photo that made the Tribune's website in minutes and its front page the next day

Mayor Harry Murphy arrived with flowers. With the support of editorials in The Call, he had defeated the incumbent in the fall elections. He declared that "This is Dunfield Call Week in our town. Thank you for being the voice of reason in Dunfield, and congratulations on bringing some fame to us."

A banner, donated by the company that printed The Dunfield Call, was erected within an hour across Main Street and read: "Home of the Pulitzer Prize-winning Dunfield Call."

Over in the corner of the Call offices, Tim and Hank sat with what looked like forced smiles.

"We have to sell, Tim," said Hank. "Even if we could secure funding to pay the legal costs for this award-winning series, we know our wives. They might take on another investigation that could yield problems from a corporation."

"Yep, you said it," answered Tim. "Gotta sell. But I do not want to think about what life will be like for us with our unhappy wives."

A month later, Janet's parents came from Florida and Kitty's dad from his Cape Cod home to join The Call staff, as well as Tim and Hank, at the Pulitzer Prize luncheon ceremony in New York. Janet and Kitty chose conservative black dresses to wear to the event, and had their picture taken with Clara and Harriet as they all accepted the award on behalf of The Call.

"I once had dinner at the home of one of my journalism professors who had won The Pulitzer years before when he was a newspaper reporter," said Janet to her tablemates, "and I asked where the prize was. He showed me. It was a certificate---not a trophy or plaque. It was sort of hidden on a wall among other journalism prizes that he had won. Wonder what we get now."

Sure enough, they got a certificate---along with $10,000.

"Wow---we can pay for this trip to New York," laughed Hank.

"But that certificate will be framed in gold," said Janet, "and displayed prominently in our offices."

That evening they were guests of Harriet and her husband at a Manhattan private club to which they still belonged, and the festivities continued until near midnight.

Stories in the national trade publications, as well as in major media outlets, detailed the dilemma faced by the small Pulitzer Prize-winning Connecticut weekly that was reeling in debt because of the prolonged libel suit it had won. Kitty and Janet were quoted as saying that the cost of the suit and appeal was in the hundreds of thousands of dollars, and that the idea of being in debt for years did not sit well with them.

"We thought about suing Lerod Health Enterprises for filing the suit against us in what we believe was its attempt to bankrupt us. But to do that we would have to fund some more legal costs and we cannot assume any more debt," Janet remarked in an Associated Press story. She explained that "the wheels of press freedom stop turning when big-dollar firms can use their resources to force out small businesses."

After a month of mulling their options, Kitty and Janet made the decision: the paper would go up for sale along with the building. They had thought of keeping the building and just selling the business but knew the economics of that approach was not viable. Any interested buyer would want to own the office space and the rest of the structure.

"I think we should advertise through press associations and trade magazines," said Janet. "We can do it ourselves without a broker. If we do need a real estate specialist later, we will work with one of those who advertises with us."

With the help of Clara and the interns, they arranged for notices of sale to be placed in the newsletters of the press groups and in other publications geared to media buyers. They made sure the copy included the information that the paper had won a Pulitzer Prize.

"Maybe that will increase its worth," said Kitty.

"It should but who is going to come to Dunfield to run a paper?" answered Janet.

They worried that one of the firms that ran online-only newspapers would take over The Call and they vowed to try and encourage a buyer to keep The Call intact with its popular print edition and online site. They realized, though, that they really had little jurisdiction over the paper's future. It was important just to get a buyer and that was the focus.

As soon as official for-sale notices were out, Kitty and Janet got a call---from CBS in New York---with a request that the pair be interviewed for the Nightly News. A reporter and camera crew arrived in Dunfield the next day and wound up interviewing not only Kitty and Janet but town officials who expressed their regrets at the thought of losing the editors/owners of The Dunfield Call to what, as Mayor Harry Murphy said, "might be outsiders who do not know this charming town." When the story was aired nationally, The Dunfield Call's online site was swamped with comments from every level of society, from journalism professors to people who hated seeing a Pulitzer Prize-winning entity in effect be penalized for engaging in good journalism.

"God, I wish we did not have to do this selling bit," said Kitty as she and Janet sipped on their favorite Chardonnay at their weekly business meeting.

"It's enough to make me stop drinking," responded Janet. "I wonder what I will be doing for my next career. Probably slinging hash somewhere."

"Well, you still have the 'Oh, Mother' column so you can continue to answer all those deep questions about the best foods for babies or dealing with the family hamster."

"The competition from blogs and online sites is really cutting into our syndication business and my column probably does not have a long shelf life. Maybe we should sell real estate."

"Well, we are already into that business as we try to sell this place on our own," said Kitty. "Frankly, I wish we would fail."

CHAPTER 34

———

JANET WAS ON A FIELD trip with Marta's third-grade class when her cell phone rang. It was Kitty.

"What are you doing right now, Jan?"

"Dealing with bones."

"Wow, Jan, are you actually making that great homemade chicken soup that your mother used to make for us?"

"No, these bones are a bit too big for the pot although a nice bowl of chicken soup sounds great right now."

"What kind of bones are you talking about?"

"Tyrannosaurus Rex."

"Oh, cripes, Janet. Are you at the Dinosaur Museum?"

"Yes, and I think we can write a column about how bone-headed we are to volunteer for something like this. The kids keep asking me questions about dinosaurs and I say 'have you seen Jurassic Park?' What do I know about dinosaurs? I should be on a class trip to a sports venue."

"Well, Miss ex-sportswriter and partner, I just called to give you a heads-up on something. Clara got a call that Jared Rockwell wants to visit our offices this afternoon."

"Jared Rockwell? Don't tell me he wants to buy the paper that his parents owned. There goes journalism. But a buyer is a buyer."

"Will you be back here this afternoon?"

"Yep, and with a gift for you."

"A dinosaur ball point pen? That is my present?" asked Kitty after Janet returned from her dinosaur foray.

"What other copy editor extraordinaire has a pen in the form of a dinosaur? Figured it is perfect since it looks as if our paper soon will be extinct."

"You are funny, for sure," laughed Kitty. "How many times have I told you that your next career should be in comedy?"

"That could be soon if we sell this place, Kitty. And I am not thrilled to think that a Rockwell would buy it."

"As they say, we have to entertain all offers," Kitty said.

"Talk about a cliché. How dumb. You entertain guests or an audience. Who really entertains offers?"

Janet broke into a rendition of "Let Us Entertain You" as Kitty joined in just as Clara called from downstairs to tell them that Jared Rockwell was on his way up to the owners' offices.

The dapper-looking Rockwell, who appeared to be around 60, walked into the office accompanied by Jack Mason, the lawyer who had represented the Rockwell family for years.

"You always sing when you work?" asked Rockwell.

"Yes, we are preparing for a new gig: The Call Girls on Broadway. Think we have a chance?"

"Maybe," said a smiling Rockwell. "Have to see how you dance first."

He then asked if he could discuss something with them and the women sat down at a conference table with Rockwell and Mason. Kitty and Janet were ready to tackle any negotiations with a prospective buyer even if they were not enthused about this one.

"We would be happy to hear you out," said Kitty. "Is it about the sale of this place?"

Rockwell looked a bit puzzled and then said: "My mother inherited this paper and she really did not know what to do with it. She sold it to you and was so happy to hear that you kept Clara on and that you really worked hard to make this such a great paper. She did not live long enough to find out that you would win The Pulitzer but she was alive during the libel case and quite upset at the way Lerod Health Enterprises treated you. You know Lerod is a public company and my mother owned stock in it and she kept telling me she would sell it because she was angry about the lawsuit."

"Did she?" asked Kitty.

"No," said Jared Rockwell. "She did something interesting with it. That is why I am here today."

Jack Mason smiled at Kitty and Janet as Rockwell continued: "We had the disposition of her will last week and Jack is the lawyer handling all of that. She left the Lerod stock to you."

"You are kidding," said Janet. "God Bless your mother. She must have had a sense of humor to leave us some stock in a company that is basically bankrupting us."

"Is the stock worth much?" asked Kitty.

Rockwell turned to lawyer Mason who looked at Kitty and Janet and said: "As of today, it is worth about two million dollars."

Silence enveloped the room. Janet and Kitty appeared to be in shock as Mason explained that "the monies you would get from selling the stock are to be used for The Dunfield Call---to cover expenses and perhaps to expand. That was spelled out in the language of the will."

Kitty was in tears.

"You mean your mother just saved us from losing our business? And she did it by making us stockholders in a company that sued us for libel after we investigated its local hospital?"

Janet headed to the refrigerator kept in a break room near the office and grabbed a bottle of Chardonnay that was being chilled for the next business meeting of The Call Girls. She returned with glasses and said: "I thought we had the high point of our careers with the Pulitzer. But this tops everything. "

"I'll drink to that," said Jared Rockwell. "And one more bit of news. Your articles pointed out that the nursing home affiliated with St. Mark's Hospital was slated for closure by LHE, and that infuriated my mother. Her sister had lived there in her last years and received great care. In fact, my parents donated the money for the patients' library there. So the Rockwell Foundation is buying that nursing home and we plan to upgrade the facilities and bring it back to its glory days when patients were the main concern, not profit."

Now Janet was in tears, too.

"I don't know what to say."

CHAPTER 35

———

THE NEWS THAT MRS. ROCKWELL had left stock to Kitty and Janet was not mentioned when the paper announced that the owners had taken the business off the for-sale market. The press release only said that the owners would use family funds to keep the operation going.

"It's a good story about Mrs. Rockwell but not now," said Janet. "Let's keep a lid on this until we get some more information about Lerod."

Her recommendation, seconded by Kitty, was to sell some of the Lerod stock to pay off the remaining legal bills but to retain some shares so they could attend the stockholders' meeting in Boston.

Several weeks later, Kitty and Janet signed into the stockholders' session at a Boston hotel. The registration team did not raise an eyebrow at seeing the names, leading Kitty to say: "We are not news here. Lerod is always into defending itself with lawsuits, it appears, and ours may have been no big deal to people who work for this company."

A week before, Janet and Kitty had studied the LHE annual report.

"This company needs some good copy editors," said Kitty. "Apparently the ones they have do not understand basic grammar. She pointed to a sentence in the report that read **'Faced with a**

decision as whether or not to build a new hospital in Elmira, N. Y., groundbreaking took place in June after the board voted to go forward with the construction."

Kitty said the sentence made it sound as if **groundbreaking** faced the decision. "Wonder how much I would get paid to be the editor of this report?"

Janet told Kitty to bag that thought and concentrate on their objective: to find out the legal costs LHE incurred for the lawsuit against The Call.

Now, as they sat in the back of the auditorium in Boston, they waited patiently for the Q and A session that followed the LHE chairman's report.

Several questions came from people who were upset by the overall spending by LHE on varied projects. One person alluded to that "lawsuit that this company lost to a paper that won The Pulitzer Prize."

The chairman never answered directly but said that he planned to watch spending in the future.

Kitty had her hand raised for awhile when she was called on.

"I read the poorly written annual report and saw the high figure representing the company's overall legal costs for the past year. Could you tell us exactly what Lerod Health Enterprises spent on the failed lawsuit against The Dunfield Call?"

The chairman looked around, apparently seeking an answer from another executive on stage. A gentleman, apparently the chief financial officer, then stood up and said: "We don't have the exact figures on that. It is just part of our legal costs."

Kitty said that a public firm must deal in transparency and asked the man to secure the figures.

The chairman said: "Fine. Where do we send that information?"

Kitty answered: "To me. Or my business partner sitting here. At The Dunfield Call in Connecticut."

The chairman said nothing, but people started to turn around and look at Janet and Kitty. One woman, who had cited her displeasure with LHE in a previous question, said out loud: "Congratulations to you two for that investigation. Finally someone is analyzing what this company does at its hospitals."

Then about 25 others stood up and applauded Kitty and Janet.

The chairman said he was not aware that any media personnel were registered for the shareholders' meeting.

Janet stood up and said: "We are registered. As stockholders."

The chairman, whose face was turning red, ended the question-answer session and walked out.

Janet and Kitty smiled.

"Cannot wait to get that information about the legal costs," Kitty said as she turned to leave the room.

A middle-aged, professionally-dressed woman approached Kitty and introduced herself as head of Lerod's corporate communications.

"How can you say that our annual report is poorly written?" she asked.

"Well, you apparently don't edit it. You use WHO instead of WHOM at least four times. You think the word data is singular. And, as for dangling participles: they are all over that report. But I am probably the only stockholder who read the report and understood those things. So if you aim for perfection---and we do at The Dunfield Call---pay for a good editor next time. Oh, here's my business card."

Janet grabbed Kitty before the discussion went any further, and they hightailed out of the hotel and to the nearest Irish pub where they saluted their performance with dark beer and fish 'n chips.

The next day, they sold the rest of their LHE stock.

CHAPTER 36

———

A FEW MONTHS LATER, WITH their business problems pretty much solved, Janet and Kitty weighed their options for celebrating their 40th birthdays.

"Heck, our high school friends are all 40 this year, so we should have a joint celebration of some kind."

Thus, they joined a dozen of their St. Agnes Academy classmates for dinner one evening at Standish Steakhouse, one of the area's top restaurants.

One by one, the women detailed how their lives had transpired to this point. Kitty and Janet both said they never figured they would own a thriving business and be recipients of such acclaim in the journalism arena.

"But motherhood is what really keeps us going," said Kitty.

"Going crazy, you mean," added Janet.

A few of the attendees were working fulltime in real estate or at large insurance companies, and another loved her volunteer work as a docent at a local museum.

Penny Wilson said little until she was asked if she was considering ever returning to teaching, her profession until she quit a decade earlier to raise her family.

"Well, I am going to work somewhere. Soon. No choice. I am getting divorced."

"Are you for real?" asked Kitty. "You and Hugh always seemed to be the model couple in the group."

"Ironically, model is a good word for the situation," she said. "He is involved with one, it appears."

"Oh, cripes, what can we do to help?" asked one of the women.

"Pray for me."

Janet looked over at Lou who was seated across the table.

"That is a job for you, Sister Louise."

"No. Not anymore."

"Not any more prayers from a nun?" asked Kitty.

"Not a nun anymore," she answered.

The whole group eyed Lou. It was at least a minute before a word was spoken—by Lou herself.

"I left the convent last week. After 22 years. Living at my parents' home until I finish law school in six months."

"Then what?" asked Penny.

"Want to get out of Connecticut and away from the order. Some of the nuns are not happy with my decision. I plan to move to Manhattan. I have a tentative job offer at a firm where my cousin works and my parents are happy to help me out."

"What did your mother say when she heard you were leaving the convent?" asked Janet.

Lou laughed.

"She said now she won't be able to retire to Blessed Mother Villa with the mothers of other nuns."

The friends all chuckled, and saluted their 40th natal days by lifting glasses of champagne.

"Let's vow that, no matter what happens, we will be here in a decade to mark our 50th birthdays," said Kitty. "And who knows what these next 10 years will bring. Let's not even try to guess."

At the end of the next day, Janet and Kitty sat in their offices and reminisced about their get-together and the many experiences they had had over the years.

Kitty started listing some events: the fake canoe race, Bermuda spring break, days at The Tribune, emergency room experiences, purchase of The Call, their adventures with their kids, their thriving NEWScamp, the lawsuit, the Pulitzer, the lollipop caper, the stock inheritance, etc.

"Unbelievable. So many things," she said, "and we are still in business after our investigation and lawsuit."

"Yes," said Janet," and we have to make sure we stay in business."

The door opened and in came Harriet Lyman.

"I have some interesting news," she said.

"Hit us with it," said Kitty.

"Well, I was in Manhattan yesterday for lunch with some of my former colleagues at the prosecutor's office and when I mentioned that I really loved living in Dunfield, they told me that they are handling a case about a Dunfield resident who is going to be charged later this week with paying off some New York City employees to get licenses for his company to do work on some buildings in the city. The lawyers think this guy also paid off some municipal authorities in a few Connecticut towns to get contracts."

"Holy cow," said Kitty. "What is this guy's name?"

Harriet Lyman smiled broadly.

"Frank McDow. Of McDow Construction. One of your least favorite people in town. And who knows? Did he pay off anyone in Dunfield or one of the other towns we cover?"

Kitty was in her glory.

"We are going to find out. That jerk who fired Tim's dad and blasted us a billion times. And was head of the St. Mark's board. We need to get on this one."

Janet threw up her hands.

"Another investigation that could get us back in court? He'd find something to sue us on. How can we take a chance on this? No way we are tackling this one."

Then she looked up at the gold-framed Pulitzer certificate on the wall in the office.

"Oh, cripes. We have a reputation to uphold. Let's get to work on this. Harriet, you interview the Manhattan attorneys and find out the details of the case there. We can run an initial story about that. Clara can track down any municipal contracts in towns around here and we can decide how to follow up. Kitty, find out if Tim knows former McDow employees who worked with his father; they might know something. Send the interns out to take photos of McDow trucks as they leave the company's facilities. I will research state laws about contracts. Let's get crackin' on this!"

The Call Girls were back in their element.

ABOUT THE AUTHOR

——————

TINA RODGERS LESHER, A NATIVE of Dunmore, Pa., is a graduate of Marywood Seminary, Scranton, Pa., and Wheeling (W. Va.) Jesuit University. She received a master's degree from the University of Missouri School of Journalism and a doctorate in English education, with a specialty in the teaching of writing, from Rutgers University.

She served as assistant women's editor of The Scranton Tribune before working as a copy editor at The Philadelphia Inquirer and The Hartford Courant. For a number of years, she handled public relations for nonprofit groups and worked as a freelance writer. She then joined the faculty at William Paterson University of New Jersey, from which she retired in 2015 and later was named professor emerita of journalism.

As a 2006-07 Fulbright Scholar to the United Arab Emirates, she researched the changing role of women in that oil-rich country. Her novel, *The Abaya Chronicles,* based on information she gleaned in her research, was named top fiction book for 2011 by the National Federation of Women.

The author and her husband, Dr. John Lesher, reside in Westfield, N.J. and are the parents of three adult children.

Made in the USA
Lexington, KY
12 November 2019